ELECTRODOMÉSTICOS

ELECTRO

SARABANDE BOOKS
LOUISVILLE, KENTUCKY

DOMÉSTICOS

STORIES MOIRA McCAVANA

This is a work of fiction. For more information about the treatment of historical
events in this book, please see the author's notes.

Publisher's Cataloging-In-Publication Data
(Provided by Cassidy Cataloguing Services, Inc.).

Names: McCavana, Moira, 1993-
Title: Electrodomésticos : stories / Moira McCavana.
Other titles: Electrodomésticos
Description: First edition. | Louisville, Kentucky : Sarabande Books, [2024] |
Includes bibliographical references.
Identifiers: ISBN: 978-1-956046-27-4 (paperback) | 978-1-956046-28-1
(ebook)
Subjects: LCSH: País Vasco (Spain)--Fiction. | Allegiance--Spain--País
Vasco--Fiction. | Families-- Spain--País Vasco--Fiction. | Autonomy
(Psychology)--Fiction. | Nationalism--Spain--País Vasco--Fiction. | Spain--
History--20th century--Fiction. | LCGFT: Historical fiction. | Short stories.
Classification: LCC: PS3613.C35692 E44 2024 | DDC: 813/.6--dc23

Cover art by Miguel Marina.
Cover and interior design by Danika Isdahl.

Printed in USA.
This book is printed on acid-free paper.
Sarabande Books is a nonprofit literary organization.

To Miguel and Madeline, eternal inspiration in art and life.

CONTENTS

You take delight not in a city's seven
or seventy wonders, but in the answer
it gives you to a question of yours.

Italo Calvino, *Invisible Cities*

RECUERDOS: GUERNICA

In Guernica, there isn't a tree, on the outskirts of town, from whose gnarled arms dangle felt berets. The hats are not a range of colors—they are not blue, cream, maroon, brown, orange, violet, or green. The hats did not begin as buds, as specks of folded felt that uncurled as the tree developed from a sapling and matured.

New hats do not sprout each spring, and if you happen to walk beneath the tree, and you find that a hat is hanging at the right height to lightly brush the top of your head, you are not just welcome to take it, to loosen it with careful force from the end of the branch, and you are not just welcome to wear it, with pride however quiet or loud, on your walk back into town.

The tree was not born from the scraps of a single beret that rode the top of a single bald head as it fled the planes that flew over Guernica, less than a year into the Civil War. Weeks after the bombs had all been dropped, and the man had separated from his hat, and separately, both had burned, the tree did not grow from the small germ of felt that had sunk into the earth.

Now, when the sun turns down on the end of the day, the tree of hats does not stand, its back to the darkening sky, like an old and benevolent puppet master, like a great keeper of the world.

It doesn't, because in Guernica, there isn't a tree. I've been honest this whole time; there are no many-colored hats, no buds that bloom. The outskirts of town are pitted with sheet metal warehouses, auto shops, and with scattered piles of sand and wood.

When the bombing took place, a whole block of buildings collapsed at the same time as the first beret-wearing men hit the ground. As the separate pieces of them—those buildings and those men—merged to unity, the berets slid straight from heads into piles of rock, and from that rock nothing grew.

NO SPANISH

When I was twelve, when we still lived in that small moldering farmhouse in the hills behind Guernica, my father outlawed Spanish from our household. Like a dictator himself, he stood at the head of our family table and yelled, "No Spanish, NO SPANISH," waving his arms as though at the helm of his own national uprising. "We will all forget about that language, is that clear?"

These demands, of course, he had delivered in Spanish, though not one of us rushed to correct him. It was evidence that he, like us, spoke nothing else. To abandon Spanish would be to abandon the language in which all of our well-intentioned but tenuous relationships had been built: it removed our field of gravity, our established mode of relating to one another. Without Spanish, it seemed entirely possible that one of us might spin out into space. How were we supposed to tell each other practical things? *Keep out of that corner; I've just spilled water and it's*

slippery. Hold the door; I have too many things in my arms. Please,
just leave me alone. Please, don't even touch me.

It's obvious to me now that for my father, this impulsive vow to
speak only in Basque functioned as a double agent: a radical act
of political defiance masked as farce. When his lips split into a
wily smile and his eyes flickered, I felt as though he were signing
us up for a ridiculous play. On that first evening I was already
calculating how soon I might be able to drop out.

Even several days into our experiment, when he banished
my brother to sleeping outside for speaking Spanish offhandedly,
we didn't believe him. My mother and I watched in silence as
he pulled my brother's bedding from his mattress, and we all
followed him around to the back of the house. Until he set my
brother's comforter down on the grass, his pillow at the head of
it, I'd been sure that he was joking.

Julen's makeshift bed was placed right beneath my window,
and I stuck my head out over him once our parents had gone to
sleep. Because their bedroom was next to mine, we couldn't risk
speaking, so instead we exchanged a series of faces, beginning
with *our father has gone crazy*. Later, after we ran out of faces to
make, and after a long period of just staring at each other, he
fell asleep. At some point, the moon came across his face, and
I watched as the lines of approaching adulthood became more
pronounced. My brother was older than me by seven years and a
few months. Sometimes I wished that he were my father.

My brother was allowed to sleep in the house the next night,
but his slip up had signaled to my father that we would need to
actually learn our new language if we were ever going to abandon

Spanish successfully. On Monday, he drove us all into Guernica to go to the market, and there he led us straight to a booth in the back where a pair of homely older women stood behind a table piled high with antique electronics. We were embarrassed by the way that my father, in his fledgling Basque, bartered with the women over the price of the various old radios that he held up before them.

"Three!" he proclaimed, with a rusted radio in hand, and one of the women responded with a sentence that sounded like pure static.

My father deflated. "Four?" he asked, innocently.

One of the women said to him, "Thank you, sir, for your efforts, but maybe we should stick to Spanish for the moment." She gestured to the radio and the few coins I held in my hand. "For doing this."

"*Me cago en Dios*," my father hissed without thinking, and immediately he brought his hands up to his mouth in embarrassment—not for the swear, but for his instinctive deference to our banned language. The light in his eyes sputtered out and he fled, walking hurriedly around the vendors, picking his feet up high to avoid crates of string beans and stacks of folded used clothing. We paid for the radio for him, choosing the most modern-looking one, and letting the woman pick through our change until she collected what she determined it cost.

I think even my mother felt like an orphan standing before those women, disturbed as I was by the momentary loss of my father and what looked like the permanent loss of a language we never realized we might have loved.

I should be clear about this: to speak Basque was against the law. Of course, in some towns the language was flaunted freely, even in the street—there was a certain social capital attached to speaking Basque, and an additional bonus, which I'm sure would translate into any language, if you could speak it without giving a damn—but it remained, in the eyes of our "leader," illegal.

How strictly the ban was reinforced varied with the ferocity of the local Civil Guard. In some places, fines piled up inside unopened mailboxes. In a town nearby, Basque lettering on certain gravestones was cemented over in the night. At schools, even, there were minor violences, like the stick to the back. But I didn't know much about that when we were in the farmhouse. On the day of his big announcement, and in one of our last conversations together in Spanish, my father explained to me only the simple overarching facts: Our leader was General Franco. Our Spain—and we—were his.

"Franco doesn't want us to speak our own language because he says that in Spain, everyone should speak Spanish," my father explained.

"Well, that makes a little bit of sense," I said. He recoiled. "Doesn't it?"

"Ana, we are our own people."

"Okay."

"A lot of people think that we should be our own country."

"Okay." He was no longer waving his arms. Instead, he'd sat back down, and was crumpling and uncrumpling the napkin in front of him.

"We can't give our language to them," he said. He was hunched over the table, the earlier bravado drained from his body. Petrified, my brother and my mother stayed in their seats, but I went to my father and put my arms around him.

I said, "It's just hard to feel like it's my language since I've never spoken it, Papi."

My father kissed the crown of my head and thumbed his clumsy fingers through my hair. I watched my mother and Julen fidget nervously across the table, and in that moment I felt like a victor for the rest of us. Then my father brought his hand to the back of my neck and squeezed, a sign of affection I always pretended to hate. We had our routine: I would bob my head furiously, attempting to free myself, while he would let out a series of squawks, transforming me into some kind of theatrical bird. If I was feeling generous, I would thrash around a bit for his entertainment.

This time the charade ended like it normally did, with my surrendering to him in a torrent of giggles, and everyone else joining in, though my father quit before the rest of us. Without moving, or raising his voice, he brought his eyes up to mine and said calmly, "*Aita*. That's what you will call me now." In his face, any sign of apology was drowned in newfound resolve.

If we had been more prudent, maybe we would have been nervous about teaching ourselves a banned language, but it was not as if we could speak enough to set the Civil Guard after us. It was not as if we could have a full conversation. For the first week or so, our pathetic vocabularies barely overlapped. I think we all assumed that at some point we would speak a word that someone else knew, and so it became a game, a test of our faith, to continue an exchange without revealing the meaning of whatever words we had spoken to the other person.

On the second or third day of our exile from Spanish, while

I was eating breakfast, my mother came into the kitchen and spoke a string of sounds that I didn't understand. When I stared at her blankly, she bobbed her head around a bit as though to say, *You know these words, don't think too hard.* I raised my eyebrows, and waited for her to surrender to pantomiming whatever she'd meant. Instead she pulled her arms into her sides as though bound in a body bag, shot a pair of raised eyebrows right back at me, and then slowly backed out of the room.

It became our silent joke, our laugh-less gag. Julen adopted it too, pinning his arms to his sides in defense when our blank reactions clued him in to the fact that he had spoken a sentence we didn't know. Imagine the stupid words we taunted each other with: "beans," "bottom," "salt," "ear," "fingernail," "onion," "sock."

By then, Julen had finished high school and I was in the middle of my summer break. During the endless stretch of those first wordless days, our hours bent around breaking each other's resolve. Even when my mother pretended to be busy frying peppers or tending to our languishing garden, she was ready to sprint after us and pry our hands from our sides if someone came up behind her and whispered *belarri*.

The day we returned from the market, my father planted himself at the kitchen table, and there, he took to repairing the radio. If we had been using Spanish, he probably would have declared something like, "*Esas malditas mujeres* . . . can you believe it? Selling me junk that doesn't even work," but after his slip up, he was careful to uphold his own rules. He suffered silently, and upon this initial bed of frustration piled up layers of small annoyances as he struggled to make any headway with the repair. Each time he thought he had made some mistake he plunged into a hysterical cough and slapped his hand against the table, as though he had crossed wires in his own body instead. We watched his strange behavior from hidden corners of the house: the top landing of the stairs; the pantry; outside, crouched beneath a window. When finally a tiny sound curled from the radio's speaker, he pounded the table so violently that he left a spiderweb of cracks in the wood.

Reluctantly, we emerged from the shadows to join him. As I neared the radio, distinct voices separated out from the static, and hung there in our kitchen as though our own familial ghosts. Even after years—my whole life—living in that farmhouse, I still think of that night as the first time that I really heard our language. My father's eyes blazed wildly in the settling darkness. My mother put a kind hand to his back, but she looked pained. We all knew it was the end of our game.

We stayed around the radio for so long that night that I fell asleep right there, beneath the table, with my head resting on my father's feet. Several hours later I woke up alone in the empty kitchen, my body splayed upon the floor.

Over the next week, we gathered for three to four hours each day to listen to the radio, attempting to absorb whatever we could. My father perched himself over a blank sheet of paper and, armed with a pen, he scrambled to copy down phrases as they spilled from the speaker. But they came out rapidly—he was left clawing after the end of the previous sentence while a new one began. And then there was the problem of no one knowing if whatever combination of letters he put to the page existed at all.

When it became clear that the radio was a failure—that it would never teach us any real Basque—my mother took to mimicking the woman that we listened to each day on the news station. Like the announcer, she would say *arratsalde on*, in a delicate female newscaster voice, and she would continue her fake broadcast, beginning with the random words that we all had learned when we finally pooled our vocabularies, then devolving into a series of ugly, made-up sounds. She once contorted her throat so extremely that she sent herself into a choking fit. Julen rushed up and smacked her on the back until she regained control, spit dribbling down her chin. My father never applauded at the end of these performances.

I have not shared any more about that early period of my childhood spent chasing my brother around the grounds of the farmhouse, but if it's important to know anything else about that time, know this: every night, the sun set behind us (it seemed like it was right behind us). And though simple, it's the truth: we were happy.

That period ended abruptly with my father's announcement that he had found himself a job at the restaurant of a nearby tavern. "They're in desperate need of a general manager." He paused, and for a moment we all understood this to mean that he was leaving us. But then he continued that there was a job for my mother too, as the hostess of the restaurant, and that he'd secured guest rooms on the third floor of the hotel upstairs for all of us. "And better yet," he went on, "the man who has hired me speaks perfect Basque, and so does the entire staff. We're offered complementary lessons every Sunday afternoon, which means that this," he said, his whole face aflame, "will be the last time you'll ever hear me speak Spanish."

Would you believe me if I told you that I hadn't even realized it? That the initial shock of the announcement distracted me completely from the language? I hadn't even recognized that he was speaking in Spanish until he mentioned it himself, but by then he had finished his announcement—at the end, I think he even bowed—and he was already silent, sitting down.

My mother and I found each other on the staircase later, after my father fell asleep, and though I suppose we could have spoken Spanish, we didn't. Julen discovered us when he got up in the middle of the night to go to the bathroom, and stayed with us until we all parted ways in the early morning.

The walls of the Ibarra Tavern were plastered with purple wallpaper that slouched away from the molding, like the last dying petals of a flower. When we arrived, a month after my father had convened us for his announcement, we were greeted by the tavern owner in the foyer, and he paraded us through the whole ground floor with our suitcases still in hand. On the tour, he spoke to us in rapid Basque, but he gestured enthusiastically enough that I assumed that I understood what he was pointing out: the range of wines on tap at the bar, the lacquered wood paneling that reached midway up the wall of the dining room, the corner of the room that could be closed off for private events, and the curtains, egg-yolk orange, that made the whole room glow as though it were the inner core of the sun when, toward the end of the day, the afternoon lent its longest beams of light to the tavern floor. In the kitchen, the new industrial-strength dishwasher, the steel countertops for food preparation, and the pots and pans that dangled from the ceiling. The profusion of eggs, milk, and meat stacked in the fridge.

Upstairs in our rooms, my father repeated one of the few phrases in Basque we had all learned from the radio, *oso ondo*, which translated literally to "very good." "*Oso ondo*," he posed to us all as though a question, and then he repeated it again to himself as he climbed into a bed that my mother had made a moment before. He whacked the mattress with both hands, grinning as they rebounded with each effort. "Very good," he squealed. "Very, *very* good!"

The next afternoon, Julen and I padded around the upstairs floors, exploring what we hadn't been shown on Mr. Ibarra's tour. From down in the lobby, we heard the distant chatter of a new group checking in. Julen pushed lightly on the nearest door and it gave to reveal a room identical to ours, with two twin beds sticking out from the wall. It was his idea to swipe the pillows from the head of the mattress, place them at the foot, and then to turn back the covers accordingly so that it looked like all the beds had been set up for guests' heads to rest where their feet should have been, to loll about exposed and defenseless in the center of the room.

When we entered the rest of the rooms to switch around the beds, they were all unoccupied, except for one at the end of the hall, where we found the tavern owner's wife, naked, her drooping body framed perfectly in the outline of the door.

To make up for our misconduct, we were given our first jobs at the tavern.

Julen worked the bar, and I worked clearing tables. The rest of the waitstaff were girls aged sixteen, maybe seventeen or eighteen, who were all friends of Mr. Ibarra's daughter, Maite, and who spoke to each other urgently in fluent Basque. They were nice enough when Mr. Ibarra introduced me, each of the five of them said *aupa* in a scattered chorus, and afterward Maite herself showed me the technique for clearing customers' plates and balancing them down the length of both arms.

When a cascade of teacups slid from my arm at the end
of my first shift, one of Maite's friends volunteered to sweep it
up. She didn't complain as she stretched the broom into the far
corners of the kitchen, collecting the shards that first escaped
her. Even before that, when the teacups were just beginning to
shatter, she'd stayed calm; she hadn't even looked at me.

In our Sunday grammar lessons with Mr. Ibarra, we began, somewhat randomly, with expressions of want: "I want, you want, he/
she/it wants." We only had access to our very small vocabularies,
and so were stuck making sentences like "I want an onion" or "I
want a shoe," but after that we learned how to pair "want" with
other verbs, and then we became able to sound our own thoughts
in the language: "I want to eat." "I want to sleep." "I want to
use the bathroom." "I want to do _____." "I want to say
_____." "I want to forget _____."

But as it turned out, "want" was not necessarily a logical place
to start. I suspect we began there only by my father's request.
I understood—it was liberating to air our wants. For a brief
moment, we felt fully formed in the language, able to express not
just our needs, but our superfluous desires. After that, however,
Mr. Ibarra sent us back to the beginning, where we belonged.
The next week, all that we were given to couple with "want" was
"I am," "it is," "my name," and "this," "that," "there," along with a
small bank of bland adjectives: "pretty," "short," "long," "small,"
"sad," "exciting," "skinny."

After our first lesson, I foolishly believed I was on the cusp
of being able to speak my own thoughts as they rose up in my
mind—something I hadn't realized I'd lost when we gave up
Spanish. Still, no matter how I toyed with that second collection

of words, they never brought me any closer to sounding like myself. And they were difficult for me, that was the tragedy. Despite the hour-long lesson with Mr. Ibarra and the additional hour I spent on my own, I couldn't figure out how "I am" changes to "you are." I felt the limitations of the language again, fumbling through those conjugations, and I lost my desire to voice even my wants.

Mr. Ibarra had us working three shifts a week, seven to midnight. Initially, my mother had stood up for me. Fifteen hours was too much, she said; I was only twelve. I never had a curfew at the farmhouse—there was no need—but if I had, it would have been well before midnight, or one in the morning when I really got off work, having pawed through a sink of dirty dishes while two of Maite's friends lazily dried the plates and returned them to their place. But when my mother brought it up, my father responded, in ill-conjugated words, that we were indebted to the Ibarras for allowing us to move to the tavern in the first place. There was nothing he could do. Mr. Ibarra was a reasonable man. He even had children himself.

It was not until my fifth shift that I learned that Maite, Mr. Ibarra's daughter, was in fact one of four Maites in the kitchen. I called her name—I needed to know what to do with the steak knives that I had just cleared—but before I finished speaking, three other girls turned around and stared at me with dull, probing eyes. Seconds later, the real Maite emerged from a corner of the kitchen with a potato skinner and a half-bare potato in hand. I held up the steak knives and the real Maite pointed to a soaking bin behind me. The other girls turned back to their work. I could never remember, later, who was Maite and who was not.

But the Maites loved Julen. That was true of all of them. After the night shifts, they emptied into the alley behind the tavern and settled on the sloping stone. They used the angle of the alley to recline comfortably in provocative poses. Someone was always lounging on her side with her head propped coquettishly upon a hand; others lay on their backs, and kept their bent legs open wide enough to make a tent of their skirts. From above, the alley would have looked an oddity: a narrow chamber of stone dotted with their soft, heaping mounds of flesh.

The first time I was invited to join, I sat a length away, on the back steps of the tavern kitchen. A blanket of smoke hung above us in the air. After ten minutes of the Maites talking around me, I got up to leave.

"Wait, Ana," someone called out after me. I stopped and swung around on the stairs. I held onto the metal railing with one hand, letting my weight fall away from it so that my body dangled before them.

"Yeah?" I said.

"What's your brother's name?"

Every night after that, all the Maites cawed after Julen until he wandered to the alley and joined me on the back steps. He accepted one of their cigarettes the first time he sat with us, but each time after that he declined. Some of the Maites tried to engage him in conversation, but his answers, by necessity and, I liked to think, by preference, were short. I felt closer to my brother when we sat together on the back stoop of the tavern kitchen. What began as a private silence, confined to our own house, turned public in front of the Maites. It felt like an honest, unpretentious show of love for each other.

Once, out there, I woke from my thoughts encased in a veil of smoke that had drifted down the hill. A girl lounging at the foot of the steps was asking Julen a question, her arm stretched out before her, and her listless fingers clasped around his ankle.

In Mr. Ibarra's lessons, I discovered all of the ways in which Basque differed from Spanish. As we continued to add new elements to our basic sentences, I began to lose my grasp on even the most basic formulations. When we started out, I could handle *onion-an*, and then *onion-an-pretty-is*, but soon that turned into *give-me-you-onion-pretty-an*, which, when I wasn't paying attention, became *onion-pretty-an-give-me-you, or-leave-I-will-do, and-not-I-will-return*.

In painful increments, the lessons revealed the full extent to which my father's whim had restructured our lives. I questioned the order of every sentence that I spoke. For a time, I lost track of the word order entirely, both because I was confused and because I didn't care, and so every sentence came out scrambled, leaving poor Mr. Ibarra stunned and embarrassed when he listened to me speak.

One afternoon, I filled in for one of Maite's friends on a lunch shift. A group of men lingered at one of my tables for hours, dolling out liquor in small doses until the rest of the dining room emptied and they remained there alone, exceptionally drunk. I watched them from behind the bar with the boy who worked when Julen and Mr. Ibarra were not around. When one of the men raised a wobbly hand for the check I started toward them, but before I reached them, he pulled the tablecloth out from under their collection of glasses and all four drunk men charged toward the door.

As I chased after them, I yelled, "TABLECLOTH-ME-IT-GIVE," then, "ME-IT-TABLECLOTH," then, "GIVE." As my legs collapsed beneath me and the men disappeared down the street with the ruined white fabric rippling out behind them, I yelled, "TABLECLOTH-TABLECLOTH-TABLECLOTH-TABLECLOTH."

We canceled our Basque lesson on the Sunday of my thirteenth birthday, and instead, the four of us sat at a table in the corner of the dining room. My father was disappointed to miss the lesson—we were becoming relatively advanced, moving on to the past tense of "to have"—and he sat there poring over his notes until my mother came in with a lopsided cake and set it down on top of them.

He scowled at her, but he pulled my head toward his and kissed my hair. "Today, you have a birthday," he said to me. Then, growing excited, he said, "Tomorrow, you *had* a birthday *yesterday*." His eyes darted around the room. "Today, we have cake—"

"Be quiet," my mother said, cutting into it. We were eating in relative peace when Julen came in carrying a birdcage with a napkin haphazardly draped over the top.

He shoved it at me and said, "For you."

My mother and I spent the afternoon sliding our fingers between the metal bars of the cage, attempting to pat the bird's head without getting nipped by its flapping beak. The bird was petite and covered in ragged feathers that it shed indiscriminately. There could have been something wrong with it, but we didn't care; my mother and I directed toward that bird all of our love.

In the hour that remained before the dinner shift, we insisted on parading it around town, and on the walk we shared the cage between us, each of us nervously holding it by the tips of our fingers. And though it was obvious, by appearance alone, that the bird was no relation to a parrot, when my mother set its cage down on my bed that night she attempted to teach it phrases, as though the bird were capable of repeating them back to her. "I have to go to the bathroom," she said. The bird stared out at both of us. "I have to go to the bathroom," she repeated, forcefully. The bird was silent.

I yelled, "I really, really, really have to go to the bathroom!"

I planned to name the bird the next morning, but I woke up to find it had escaped from its cage and was lying in a wreath of its own feathers on the floor.

My mother had to work at the tavern that afternoon, and so Julen and I were the ones to bury the bird. We wandered the town looking for the right place to perform a burial, but in the end we decided not to bury it at all, but instead to leave it in the dumpster behind the cobbler's shop. Julen swaddled the bird in discarded leather clippings.

We felt silly for bringing it over in the birdcage when we were left carrying the empty cage back across town.

My brother left us, six months into our time at the tavern, for an apprenticeship at a tailor's shop in downtown Bilbao. He had been looking for a full-time job for weeks, and while he could have easily picked one up at the tavern, he didn't.

We each mourned his absence in different ways. My mother's pantomimes grew limp; she could never be properly funny after that. My father doubled up on Basque lessons with Mr. Ibarra. I started hanging around with the Maites until two or three in the morning, thinking of them, increasingly, as my own siblings. Maybe we had all spun out of orbit. Or maybe Julen had, and we, in the aftermath, each used it as an excuse to drift a little farther out.

A few weeks after Julen left I started going to the clandestine Basque-language school that Maite and her friends attended. Mr. Ibarra signed me up, and he drove me there on my first day. The school was housed inside an old textile factory just outside of town. Its sheet metal sides had rusted to the shade of dirt, and on the outside it bore no markings.

Inside, Mr. Ibarra led me through a hall of makeshift classrooms to a group of students who looked at least two years younger than I was. During the lunch break I left the building and stood out on the grass behind the school. I thought I would need the time to cry, but I waited for a while, and it turned out that I didn't. At some point, a cloud of birds burst across the sky. I watched as they neared each other then separated in turns, and I spent the rest of the lunch hour wishing my own bird were still alive.

Later, when I returned to the building, I caught a glimpse of Maite going up the stairs between class sessions, though she hadn't been in the car that morning when Mr. Ibarra had driven me to school.

Initially I was furious with Mr. Ibarra for having placed me in a class of eleven-year-olds, but within a few months, my Basque flourished. At some point I understood the majority of what the Maites fired back and forth between each other, and I began to chime in in little ways: "You're right, he's a turd!" or "Pass me a cigarette," or, when in doubt, "Yes, yes, yes. Yes. Yes—totally."

Eventually I moved from the back steps to the alley with the rest of them. It happened seamlessly. I didn't try any seductive poses but I did note my own pooling flesh upon the cobblestones and the growing downhill tow on different parts of my body over the course of the nights that we spent there.

Gabriel, the other barman at the tavern, took over Julen's old shifts. Though he would join us outside after work, he was soft-spoken and withdrawn. If one didn't know him, they could honestly confuse him and his chaste shyness for a specter haunting the place.

But he was also nice to me. Out in the alley, we spoke to each other in slow sentences. The Maites lounged around us and we carved a void in the flood of their ceaseless chatter. When he talked, I could see through his skin to each muscle in his face at work. When he listened, the dormant muscles spasmed at random, revealing the places where they lay otherwise hidden.

The night I visited the quarry with the Maites, I was the last one cleaning up in the kitchen. When I emerged I found a pool of people milling in front of the stoop and, as my eyes adjusted to the darkness, I saw the full assortment of Maites were there—girls who worked only one or two other shifts with me, whose faces still stood out as foreign.

The real Maite hovered at the top of the hill, detached from the group. When I shut the door to the kitchen, she turned and began walking, and the rest of us followed her up and out of the alley. I asked the girl nearest to me where we were going but I didn't understand her answer.

"The quarry," Gabriel cut in from behind me. I shook my head. "Where they dig for rocks."

He described the rock nearby as a raw piece of meat: blood red, roped with streaks of white. When I made a face, Gabriel shook his head. "No," he continued, "it's beautiful. It got so popular that they overdrilled it. They went down so deep one day that they hit a water supply."

After a long time, the road declined, and we sunk down the mountain. Somehow I emerged at the helm. The Maites descended the road behind me, the whole group of them dispersed up the hill. I still remember the drone of the car engine as it approached the sharp bend ahead, its swinging headlights as it came upon us, and after the real Maite yelled *Move* back to her friends, I remember the light striking them in their white summer clothes as they idly cleared the street while the car sat there, stranded. Still, I can't decide if, caught in the blinding sweep of those beams, the girls appeared criminals unmasked, or if the swing of their skirts as they left the road rendered them a suite of doves disbanding.

At the quarry, everyone stripped down to their underclothes, and our excess shirts and pants and dresses lay heaped in piles on the sand. At the far end of the swimming hole, a wall of stone stretched high up into the sky. It was impossible, in the dark, to tell whether or not it was red.

I went into the water with everyone else, but it was cold, and the bank dropped off quickly. When I saw a cigarette light up somewhere along the sand, I swam back to join them. One of Maite's friends nodded to me and exhaled as I settled down beside her. We lounged alongside each other, then she said, "How deep do you think it is?"

"I don't know," I said. "It drops off fast." She was silent.

"Have you been in?"

Out in the swimming hole, orphaned heads glossed the water's surface. I'm sure they were talking to each other, or they were laughing about something, but the threat of the stone wall that rose above them canceled all their sound.

"Twenty-five meters," she said. She tapped the tip of her cigarette against a rock. "That's how far down they drilled before they hit the water." When she brought the cigarette back to her mouth she looked at me for a brief moment, and she said, "No. I never go in."

One by one, other bodies surfaced and joined us up on the sand. "Hey," Maite's friend whispered. She nudged me, then motioned toward Gabriel splayed out in his boxers. "Are you guys going to kiss or hold hands or what?"

I fake-slapped her like we were real friends.

"Okay, okay," she said. "But what are you going to do? You like him, right?"

I shrugged. Stretched out and bent at odd angles, Gabriel's spidery legs glowed.

"You like him." She was talking louder now. "So go do something, don't waste your chance. There are some trees over there." She gestured somewhere behind us. Gabriel had obviously heard her, and he looked over.

"Look," She grabbed one of my shoulders and pointed to him. "He wants to go off with you too." Gabriel had already gotten up and started loping over when she called out to him, "You want to, don't you?" In response, Gabriel said nothing. He just continued nearing, the whole time smiling at both of us.

He led me into the trees, and we stumbled through branches for a couple of minutes until we could barely make out the edge of the quarry. When I strained my eyes I could just see the tip of the girl's cigarette flying about in the air. Gabriel put his back to a tree and stared into me affectionately. I realized how little I knew him.

"Come closer." He grasped my arms. He whispered, "What do you want me to do?"

I don't know how else to explain it: the question struck some dormant reflex. I answered instinctively, as though I had always planned to say to him, "I want you to speak Spanish to me."

He was silent. In the dark, I watched the familiar tremor of his muscles. He tried, "*Así?*" Like this? I nodded, and signaled for him to keep going.

"What do I say," he asked, in Basque. I shrugged. I could already feel my body growing loose with desire. I waved my arms, to say *continue*.

It's not important what he said in the forest behind the quarry, whatever stories he told with poise and animation almost embarrassing to witness. I barely registered the words as he spoke them. I dropped to my knees and listened to him like a child. I may have started crying when I heard the word *cucharilla*, unless it was instead the word *caserío* that set me off. I may even have even laid myself totally and completely on the ground.

When we emerged from the trees, the Maites were all collecting their clothes and getting ready to leave. For a while, Gabriel's clammy hand held the tip of my fingers, but at some point they let go. When we reached the tavern, I slid inside without saying goodnight to him and I felt no remorse for allowing him to walk alone to the far reaches of town. Upstairs, I tried to recover the words that he spoke and I realized I had never really heard them. I had listened only for their rhythm, for the shallow aesthetics of them. Alone in my room I had nothing to hold onto except the fading memory of their sound.

Gabriel began leaving me little presents around the tavern.

First, he left me a bag of almond cookies that his mother had made, my name written in careful, feminine handwriting across the front. I discovered them on one of the empty tables in the dining room on my way to the staircase. Some time later I found a silver bracelet on the corner of the counter where I normally helped with prep work. There was no note, but I felt confident in my assumption; a bracelet had been found on the floor of the dining room the day before. The next week I received a random assortment of glass beads, then a collection of tea bags, a patterned matchbook, a pile of loose stamps.

I wasn't purposefully avoiding him, but I wasn't spending my nights out in the alleyway either. When I heard him go down to the basement to restock the liquor cabinet at the end of our shift, I would dart past the bar and up the stairs to my room.

One Sunday afternoon when my parents were downstairs in their usual lesson with Mr. Ibarra, Gabriel knocked on the door to my room.

"Ana," he called. "I know that I'm annoying you, but please let me give you one last thing."

I hadn't expected to feel nervous around him, but when he stood there before me I saw him again in his boxers, me again, in my underwear, on the ground. He apologized for his other gifts, and I told him not to be stupid, that they were very nice. He said no, that they weren't right. What he should have given me from the beginning was this: he produced a small, used radio from his bag.

"So that we can listen together," he said. "In Spanish."

The radio wasn't the same model as my father's. In fact, Gabriel's looked totally different, but it prompted my first thought of that radio in more than a year. I got caught up in assessing how each of its features compared to the original, whose body, I realized then, I had committed to memory. When I didn't respond, Gabriel said, "Spanish, remember?" His face thawed into that same, timid smile.

I knew it was unkind to take the radio from Gabriel, thank him, and tell him I couldn't listen that afternoon. I was sorry when I closed the door on his sinking expression, but there was nothing else I could do. When I set the radio on my bed, the hefty mechanical weight of it sunk into the mattress and sprouted a crown of pleats in my covers. The whole time, I thought, it could have been that easy: I could have nudged the needle past the covert station that broadcast in Basque, and I could have found Spanish waiting there on any channel.

I could have pulled a pair of my father's shoes from the closet while my parents remained in the dining room downstairs cycling through their slow-growing vocabulary and diligently practicing the construction of conditional clauses. I could have put the radio on the bed, laid my head on those shoes, and listened for hours. And if I arranged it all right, maybe the year would have bent back on itself, delivered me back to the kitchen in our old farmhouse, and maybe my father would be there, waving around his arms, saying, "We will all forget about Basque, is that clear?"

Maybe my brother would be there too, coming in through the back door, his arms wound around a tangle of sheets and a comforter. Maybe they came straight from the clothesline, clean from my mother's scrubbing, dry from a night hung out in the mid-August air.

MASTER OF ALL SUBJECTS

The teacher's husband had been missing for two weeks, and everyone imagined this caused the teacher immense grief. Of course, you couldn't tell—she continued to take midmorning walks around the port as though her husband were still out at sea, his return promised by ritual—but people feared, we all did, that one day the boats might begin their daily caravan into the harbor and she would recognize for the first time that they did not bring him with them.

I know that during those weeks I felt a certain anxiety stir up in me at the end of the day, when the sun dipped into the sea, and in its long, pinkish light, the last of the fishermen repeopled the docks with themselves and their fish. I looked for the silhouette of her crooked figure haunting the sea wall. I held her with my eyes.

The truth was she had been a teacher for only a short time, despite her age: old, and already much past motherhood, though she had never had any children of her own. She left her position at the school abruptly, after just four or five years, we calculated, and though rumors of the reason for her departure floated around at the time (adultery? An allergy to the janitor's cleaning solution?), enough years accumulated since then that speculation had long fallen from people's minds. The irony of her unexpected departure was that, in the aftermath, she would always to us be the teacher, despite no longer teaching, whereas the other women who taught at the school remained themselves: Ainhoa Ondarra, Itziar Lozano, Amparo Zabal.

But she also merited the title; no one would deny her arduous dedication to the profession. If you encountered her in the harbor, you couldn't make it past her without enduring an explanation of the calcium content in the stone beneath your feet: the exact ratio of silica to sand. And, though she had been a teacher of chemistry, in her extended retirement she picked up cursory knowledge of all subjects previously foreign to her. If you happened upon her at night you might receive a detailed lecture on the effect of the current lunar phase on the tides, and the fish you could expect to eat tomorrow based on what the fishermen would find in those tides. Or an explanation of which constellations were currently cast across the sky. Or the name for the ancient Greek god of the sky: Ouranos.

In the evenings, when my friends and I scrambled up the mountains behind the port, I sometimes thought about her. Other women, too, flitted across my mind as we climbed and the horizon rose with us: the neighbors or classmates I thought I might one day love. And so it always struck me with surprise when, between Ibai or Andoni talking about who he was dating, the teacher's figure ghosted to the surface of my thoughts.

We spent most nights up there, in the hills, where we could get ourselves contentedly drunk without the reprimands of our fathers, who, down in the port, could do the same without having to do so in front of us, their sons. When the sun buried itself in the sea and night dropped down to us, we became a moving constellation of lit cigarette tips, and I liked the knowledge that if I lit up, or if I extinguished my tip, the group would change with me. There were eleven of us altogether, but some I was closer to than others.

I'm telling you this because I hope you might still trust me as a friend, a confidant, when I disclose that up in those mountains was where I saw the teacher's husband the night that he went missing, lying lifeless under a bush. I won't tell you the state of his body, because that I don't want you to know, friend, but I will tell you that the soft pink tip of his tongue poked out of his mouth, as though it sought one of the crude mountain berries that hung above his head.

Neither will I name the boys who in the dark pulled back the branches to reveal him to me, but I will say they carried in their hands the things that proved they had done it—you would know too, if you had seen the body—and when they let the branches swing back on his leaking abdomen some of us whistled, and some of us clapped, and some of us said nothing but erected a small cross for the man in the back mountain slopes of our mind.

They were the same boys, it turns out, who declined the teacher's invitation to have lunch with her when, a few weeks after her husband's disappearance, she invited us, her former students, to come eat at her home. We were all spooked. One person vomited down the banks of his mother's front garden when he discovered the envelope on the front step. In the end, a few of us responded to her invitation saying we would come, but when the afternoon arrived I found myself sitting alone on the bowed, blue couch in her living room.

Immediately, my brain contorted itself with anxiety. Somehow I became convinced that being there in that house felt like being inside of a lung, whether hers or my own, I couldn't tell. I knew only that one of us had intruded on the other and now we were both trapped inside of the consequences.

A small bouquet of tea bags steeped in the teapot between us. The water slowly bled brown. And then she began to teach. She took me through the origin of every artifact in our immediate vicinity. Her sentences were glacial, deliberately didactic, as though she were teaching a person new to the world.

"This vase—you know what sort of pottery I mean by 'vase,' don't you—was hand-painted with a natural cerulean pigment— do you know what color it is that I am referring to?"

Though she began with confidence, her voice, as it drew me through the room, started to splinter. The final letters of words fell off, then entire phrases dropped out of her speech until you got the sense that her true sentences forked at the base of her throat, and one half exited, while the other turned back to sit inside of her. What few words she spoke now were near a whisper:

"The beams . . . make this home . . . collected by a man . . . José Mari."

As her speech thinned, her illustrative gestures grew increasingly theatrical. With a grace painful to witness, she pantomimed the construction of the eaves above us as tears pooled in her eyes.

"Inside the beams . . . wood." Her arms swooped lengthwise to suggest a swathe of lumber. I nodded. "And inside wood . . ."

I waited. "Hemicellulose . . . coniferyl aldehyde . . . lignin-carbo-hydrate bonds . . . complex compounds . . . atoms." She stopped, then looked up at me. "Do you remember how to bond together atoms, Jon?"

Well, what could I tell her? That we never, for a second, paid attention to her lessons in chemistry class? That when we were fourteen we were already scheming, some of us, for ways to dip our hands into the local faction of Euskadi Ta Askatasuna, and that this, for us, weighed in our world more than the dynamics of a dihydrogen bond? I would have had to tell her, of course, that we had very little understanding of what ETA even was. We—I should say my friends—did what they thought they had to do in order to be noticed by them, desired by them. It goes without saying that no one emerged from any shadowy corners of the port to reveal that they were impressed with us.

Through her window I could see a small triangle of ocean, and there I imagined several hours into the future—the boats rolling inward—and two weeks into the past—her husband's body pressed to the bow, coming in with them. And I told her the truth, that no, I did not remember a single thing.

RECUERDOS: URDAIBAI

The river threaded all of Urdaibai together. From the eye of Guernica, the river bled out into the valley, sliding through the crease in the earth to the sea. It linked our towns too: the sprawling stunted apartment buildings of Forua on the western side, to the eastern Kortezubi, where the crumbling farmhouses seemed on the verge of recombining with the mountains.

It was where I learned to swim.

The way that the river curved sharply then opened at the mouth reminded me of the crook of a seagull's wing. In my earliest swimming days, when I stuck to the still, protected water on the backside of the sandbar beach, I first recognized the shape in the outline of the bay: I caught a flash of it through the rear window of my parent's car at the end of the day, when we rose home into the hills. That afternoon, when I got tired of feeling like I was drowning, I had spent the remaining hours flinging myself over the sand, chasing after birds with wings of that same shape.

You had to leave at night to fish for eels. Not in the false darkness of early morning—you were not fishing for bass, or cod, or hake—but at the peak of the bowed spine of the night you would collect your keys, your net, your lantern, and leave. You wanted a whole pool of hours to spend down there in the darkness: the time to wade until the water hit your knees and the time to wait there, the long pole of your net extended before you as though it were a third arm. If you were patient, the eels would rise to the light from your lantern, and their slim transparent heads would prick the surface. Their helpless tails ploughed the water. I always wanted to hold them.

My father had a habit of going back to the river at night, I found out when I was thirteen. I wish I could say it felt like anything besides betrayal. The first night that I caught him leaving, I had been lying folded up in my window frame because I couldn't sleep. From up the hill, the water was black and slow-moving like mud. Like it was wild, or gross, or somehow at the same time, both. The engine of our car sent a murmur out below my window. A door clapped. Then our yellow sedan slid into the street. My father's net, too unwieldy to rest in the backseat, extended out the passenger window, as he moved through the dark and away. As far as I understand now, at that point he was going every night.

Later, when I was older, I was fumbling around with a boy in the bushes that bordered the back of our property when I heard the familiar sounds of my father returning from a night of fishing. Up until then, what I had most feared was that the *jabalí*—the mountain boar that we sometimes heard grunting from above—might come down the mountain to us, but as the car neared and I heard the rattle of the motor and the rustle of gravel reshuffling itself under the weight of the tires, I saw what would happen: his headlights carving through the bushes to bas-relief our panicked bodies.

But before I could fit my shirt back over my head, the car came around the corner with its lights completely extinguished. We had sold our yellow sedan for a used black hatchback that my father preferred, and in the moments before he opened the door and dragged his net and lantern with him, the dark car sat in our driveway like a misplaced shard of sky, my father—that night—in it.

My father never brought eels into the house, and so I assumed he never followed through on the final step of fishing them: when their heads appeared at the surface, I imagined he never swept his wide and shallow net beneath them, or, if he did, I imagined he held them there only briefly before plunging them mercifully back into the water.

When I was a child my father explained to me that our eels are born in a small patch of ocean, far into the Atlantic, off the coast of Bermuda. They spend the subsequent years fleeing and returning to that same spot; the first trek across the Atlantic to reach our rivers, the second, near the end of their lives, to leave them. When the caravan into the river begins in the spring, thousands of eels cruise the currents of those shallow waters. If you lowered your lantern to the surface at night, you would find them there, coursing, like an endless, spectral fleet.

Of course, there was no way to know if you were fishing in the same group of eels, but if you moved yourself several paces down the river each night, you could certainly trick yourself into the sensation that you remained among fish you knew, and who knew you. Typically, you would fish them on their entrance into the river, when they were young, so small they were wormlike, and clear.

And so I was surprised, when I began following my father down to the river at night, to find him trailing them in the opposite direction. For nearly two years, we accompanied the dying eels on their exodus, all the way from the source of the river to the sea. I made sure to stay hidden from view, always keeping a kilometer, maybe two, behind him. He trailed his own fleet, I trailed mine.

You could see all of Urdaibai this way. Past Kortezubi, you came to Kanala, and on its stony shoreline you might find a nude bather baring their body to the world. Farther down, the bank bent to cup a mass of boats moored over a patch of rocks. You might hear improvised songs rise from tents that dot the campground cleaved to the chest of the mountain, and you might smell the scent of roasted chicken leaking from the campground's mess hall.

Across the river, at Mundaka, you might be able to make out the old casino, hunched over the port. The Church of Santa Catalina, too, which sits on a cliff above the water, might inevitably prick your vision: its gray stone walls the wind has scraped of all their color.

Then, down past Kanala, looking from my side of the river, you could see across to Bermeo and the large commercial barges that swallow up the harbor. But at this point, the river, already several kilometers ago, will have released itself to the sea, your eels with it.

86 WAYS OF BECOMING JUAN MANUEL BERASTEGUI

There are people who, for whatever inscrutable reasons, have wished that *they* were Juan Manuel Berastegui. Alright. Here is how to become him:

1. Plan your first attack:
2. Dismantle part of the railway track in Guipuzkoa, on July 18, 1961.
3. Though you'd hoped the train would derail, it doesn't.
4. Wonder if you should have been more forceful—in your mind, wield a gun.
5. Unintentionally bruise your wife's hand by squeezing it too hard, in bed, in the aftermath of these fantasies.
6. Start hearing rumors that the Civil Guard is aware of your identity.
7. Start feeling a faint sort of pain above your heart when planning the next demonstration.

8. Stop squeezing your wife's hands: she needs mobility for slicing peppers and other vegetables.
9. Start sleeping alone.
10. Start waking up in the middle of the night to massage your heart.
11. *Ilargi-argiarekin beldurtzen hasi.* (Start becoming afraid of the moonlight.)
12. In 1966, begin to teach yourself how to construct a bomb, but when the product is little more than half-complete, leave it under your bed. Leave the house.

In Guernica, Gonzalo made his bed in the barracks of the Civil Guard. That morning, he would leave the compound. He had noticed the general at the base eying him when he lingered in his bunk after siesta, only getting out of bed once all the other men had disappeared. He took his uniform off for his nap—so that it wouldn't crease—and then he lingered delicately over the buttons in reclothing himself. In the morning too, he stretched his tasks out like this, so much that the number of hours he spent on patrol collapsed down to a fraction of what they were intended to be: four before lunch, three after siesta.

He was new at the base. He had been hired all the way from his home in Valladolid, miles outside of the Basque Country, and so Gonzalo had traveled to Guernica under the impression that his duties were urgent. The man who called him about switching his Civil Guard post had sounded so fraught over the phone that when Gonzalo accepted the position he felt as though he were repairing a ruptured union. When he arrived at the barracks, his belongings slung from either arm in heavy sacks, he was surprised to find the compound bustling, already full. The man who greeted him, the assistant to the general at the base, at first barely recognized Gonzalo's name. He could see the assistant's mouth working to make it through that combination of letters for the first, or maybe second, time.

Gonzalo assumed he had been hired as part of the base's counter-terrorism efforts, and countless times in the days before leaving, he had imagined himself bursting into a roundtable meeting of ETA insurgents. He became enchanted by the thought of the men all dropping their guns on command—the synchronized fall of a crescent of weapons—and he went to sleep listening to the imagined dispersion of metal on wood. It became to him the sweetest, most comforting sound.

Only once he arrived at the barracks did Gonzalo learn that the job might be more mundane than his fantasies. He had been hired to take up someone else's former post, and so rather than leading the offensive, he would be nothing more than a regular Civil Guardsman on foot patrol.

"Watch out," the assistant said on one of his first days at the compound. "The ones you overhear making those sounds are terrorists." He slipped into a sly smile, paused then said, "Maybe not yet, but soon. They'll be figuring out how to make bombs from the horse shit behind their house." He lit a cigarette. They were outside, leaning against the back wall of the compound, on Gonzalo's first afternoon at the barracks. The assistant smoked with ease. "I'm not wrong."

Gonzalo spent his initial days at the compound in training with two other new officers. He had been a Civil Guardsman in Valladolid, and so he knew everything about general patrol—the different tiers of emergencies, how to fasten his protective vest—but he kept himself from dozing off, hoping at the start of each new session that this time he might finally be trained for some new role. Maybe, he thought, there would be extra training for some kind of counterterrorism squad. If he went, perhaps he could lobby for a promotion. On the second day, he accidentally scratched a red line up his arm in suspense.

After the fourth and final day, however, he had learned nothing that he hadn't known before. That night, he ate dinner in the mess hall with the other men who had undergone training with him, and he solemnly sipped his beer. One of them—Ángel—was large and muscular and, Gonzalo thought, was bound to be the most successful informant of the three. When he lifted the beer to his lips, Gonzalo's own slender wrists appeared deformed and frail through the murky glass.

The next morning, when Ángel and the other men left the barracks to go on patrol, Gonzalo went around to the back of the compound, to see if he could find the assistant. He planned to ask him what, exactly, he was supposed to do, but when he got there he found the cracked concrete patio empty. A fly buzzed about his head and perched in his hair. Gonzalo counted the hours until lunch.

13. Board the train that will take you across the border, into France. At Irun, transfer to Paris.

14. In the train car, gently tip your head against the edge of sleep.

15. Hope that if anyone comes looking for you and goes sifting through your bedroom, they will at least appreciate what you left them: only half a bomb still needs to be made.

16. In Paris, get off the train.

17. Spend your first afternoon on the soiled banks of the Seine, with the fishing rod that you bought at the corner store for several francs.

18. Hang the rod above the water and wait for a pull on the line.

19. Remember the morning spent at the far end of Zorrotzaurre when you caught two dozen fish within an hour, loaded them into sacks on either side of your bike, and cycled home through the shadows of the shipyards in the industrial quarter. You dumped those sacks on your kitchen table. Something happened—you were late for a meeting, impossible to be sure which one. Remember returning home hours later to find the fish had slid from the bag, and they lay spread out and dead on your kitchen floor. Remember sweeping up their ruined little bodies.

20. Ignore your panic as the night settles over you like a soft blue coat.

21. Try and fail to have any clue where you are.

22. *Pixkanaka-pixkanaka iluntasunak itotzen zaituen moduari kasurik ez egin.* (Ignore the way the darkness drowns you, bit by bit.)

. . .

23. Wake up to the prodding of a group of young boys. Try to make sense of the few words they exchange in French.

24. Watch, from your place of half sleep, one boy shoo the rest away, down the river, and hear him say to you that you should not waste your time fishing in the Seine. The water is too polluted. All the fish have died. See him gesture to your rod.

25. Say thank you to the boy and watch him return to his friends. Put his age at thirteen, possibly fourteen.

26. Feel embarrassed when he comes down the riverbank later that afternoon to find you fishing again. Consider apologizing.

27. Have the following conversation:

> BOY: Are you homeless?
> YOU: I have a place to live in another city.
> BOY: Your French is very bad.
> YOU: Thank you.
> BOY: I came back because I thought you were homeless.
>
> (*beat*)
>
> BOY: Can I offer you a place to sleep?

28. Answer the boy yes, you would live in the vacant basement of his mother's apartment building, if he was offering it. Only for the short term, because you feel strange taking something from a young boy.

29. The boy's name is Antoine. Learn how to pronounce Antoine.

The day Gonzalo decided he would leave the barracks, he stood, sweating, in the frame of the front door, and watched people moving about in the town. On the afternoons he'd spent kicking around the grounds, he had searched aimlessly for the assistant, acting on some unfounded belief that he, like Gonzalo, did nothing but circle the compound at all hours of the day. Finally, the day before, when Gonzalo was on the patio behind the building, he spotted the assistant deep in the back countryside. He was standing in the middle of the river with his pant legs rolled up to the knee, smoking. He wore large military sunglasses, his expression unreadable, and he lifted his right hand only a hair in acknowledgment of Gonzalo.

As he crossed the street and moved away from the compound, Gonzalo hoped that maybe in the town he might run into the assistant, and that the assistant might yank Gonzalo aside and greet him as he had once before, when he'd been very drunk after dinner: *My shit! My brother!* That hope dissipated as he tentatively made his way around the perimeter of the town, and all shades of familiarity—the buildings and cross streets he could see from the barracks—fell away. And anyway, the assistant, he thought, otherwise greeted him neutrally, his face barely changing in recognition of Gonzalo's own, passing right in front of him.

On this preliminary orbit around the town, Gonzalo was struck by the strange beauty of the apartment buildings in Guernica. The buildings were new—rebuilt after the bombing—and while their scuffed plaster facades appeared already wearied, somehow, when Gonzalo took them in, they aligned into a pleasing unity. The baskets of red and pink summer flowers erupted from the faded buildings like happy little wounds.

The several fragments of Basque that he overheard on the walk sounded this way too: vibrant bursts of vowels sprouted forth from those sharp, staccato words. None of the individual sounds, when spoken together, cohered into any sort of meaning. Gonzalo rolled them around in his mind as he returned to the barracks to linger in bed before lunch.

When he rose from his siesta that afternoon, he made his bed, like always, while the rest of the men filed out. He reached for his uniform, but then instead of pulling his pleated guardsman pants over his boxers, he folded them delicately, and placed them under his pillow. From beneath his bed he fished the crumpled chinos he had worn on the train from Valladolid, and over his sagging white undershirt, he buttoned the polo he found balled up in the forgotten pants. When he left the compound, he felt borne with an elastic sort of resilience.

Once in town, he went directly for the middle streets, the dense central area that he had consciously evaded that morning, when he'd been laden with the uniform. The buildings grew closer together. He passed a single café, and then a trio of them, one after another. Outside, a group of women pressed themselves up around a cluster of tables. Several balanced babies on their laps, the infants' tiny hands pawing after the bowl of nuts. Nearby, two children ran races to dip their fingers into the fountain at the end of the block. Used napkins flapped about their ankles like errant, dirty flowers. More of those nonwords flitted between them. *Hadn't they been banned?* Gonzalo grew tense.

He made his way to the end of the sidewalk then turned down a gently sloping street lined with bars. The scent of smoke and frying eggs hung in the air. Outside each bar a mass of tables and chairs were dispersed haphazardly, so it was impossible to know which tables belonged to which locale. Clustered around them were bands of women just like the first group Gonzalo passed.

He made it to the end of the street once, then circled around before starting down the block again. A small group of older men walked ahead of him. They moved languidly, despite all of them depending on walking canes. In a strange identical fashion, each of their bulblike heads drooped over their shoulders, causing what Gonzalo thought must be a dangerous curve in their spines: he felt the limits of his own physical capacity as he mimicked their steps.

A woman passing from the other direction turned to Gonzalo and said, *"Agur,"* which sounded like it meant hello, though a man at the compound had told him it meant goodbye. He blushed and dropped his head, and then the men went into a bar on the right and Gonzalo followed them.

Inside, the barroom was a cavern of dark wood. A stained glass window shed a small patch of pale green light onto the floor. Gonzalo positioned himself at the corner of the counter. The men settled down at the other end, away from him. He ordered a beer by pointing at the tap, and then he floated into a trance. Sounds from the men's conversation came into his brain, but he never wrestled with them. He never fondled them for meaning. They stacked up in his brain, and he felt full. Contentedly full.

"Zer berri, anaia?" Gonzalo refocused his eyes. One of the men had turned to him. The man spoke again, *"Zer moduz zaude? Esan dut."* Gonzalo stared back at the men. The warmth fled from him. He said nothing.

The bartender laughed, gestured toward Gonzalo, and said, *"Sartu denetik ez du hitzik esan."* Another man from the group yelled, *"Mutua da."* Gonzalo tried not to move. A cluster of dead trees hung over a corner of the town, close to the barracks, where the salt water from the marshland infiltrated their roots. The assistant had explained this to him on the first afternoon they smoked together, and now Gonzalo's own body flashed before him as a petrified trunk. He saw his legs, where they hung from the barstool, as cracked, arid stumps—"*Mutua da*," someone cawed again from the crowd—and his arm, draped over the bar, like a rigid, twisted branch. The men blew up in laughter.

Gonzalo closed his eyes.

30. Answer the door when Antoine comes to check on you on the evening of your third day in the room beneath his mother's apartment.

31. Answer Antoine when he asks you why you fled Spain with a single backpack. (Consider saying "It was an urgent departure, no time to pack." Actually say, "Packing light has been better for my back, historically.")

32. Wonder if the bomb has been completed and then decide not to tell Antoine that you have done things like teach yourself how to construct bombs.

33. Allow Antoine to come back again the next night. Allow this to repeat for several months.

34. One of these times, let him hold your fishing rod.

35. Let Antoine teach you how to fish:
    i. Pull worms from the grass in the park.
    ii. Put the tips of their tails through the hook: load as many as you can.
    iii. Lower the rod into the water and whisk it around on the surface. The fish will see your worms then.
    iv. More worms equal bigger fish.
    v. When you feel the first bite, reel in the fish with as much strength as you have.
    vi. You might need someone behind you to put his arms around your waist, if the fish is too big.

This has happened before (and it might have the unintended effect of growing your slender biceps larger).

36. Wait until Antoine exhausts his instructions. Give him two minutes of silence after he tells you, "That's it, that's how you fish," and his face hardens into a boyish sort of seriousness, before you call his bullshit.

37. Ignore his protests as you take back the rod.

38. Ask him if he wants to learn how to fish.

39. Lead him to the door of your apartment as he tells you that he has fished not one, but two million times before, in the sea and in the small pond outside the vacation cottage in Mesnil-Saint-Père he rented with his mother.

40. Ask him if he knows how to get to the train station from your apartment.

41. Tell him to meet you outside the building at a quarter past five the next morning.

42. Let him say the beginning of "*Non, putain!*"—fuck no—"That's too early" before you close the door.

43. Pull down the shades in your apartment, shutting out the moon.

44. Watch the darkness breed in the corners of the room.

Gonzalo left the barracks in his uniform. He crossed the street with confidence. The day before, he waited until everyone in the bar stopped laughing—until the men grew tired of him and looked away—to drop several coins on the counter and escape. He was armed with the basic words now: over dinner he meekly mentioned that the sounds still slid through his ears without cohering, and immediately, the other guardsmen launched their own narrow vocabularies across the table. With what seemed like real joy, they stitched together whole sentences in the air. Gonzalo felt as though he finally carved a channel into the language: *Agur*, it turned out, was "goodbye," but also "hello," in passing. *Tabernan kalea* was "the street of bars." *Kaiku atzerritarra* was "foreign idiot."

He made it to the center of town quickly, retracing his steps from the day before. Today he would police that language: as a doubly trained Civil Guardsman, it was the least he could do. He might even make an arrest. He walked with new urgency and the first few people that he came upon went silent. A young boy, who looked barely emerged from infancy, waddled by with a dog in tow. Then a single middle-aged woman passed, pushing a sleeping baby in a stroller. Gonzalo looked at her, but the woman looked down. A triangle of men came up the street, and the sharp sounds of Basque carried forward to him.

"Excuse me," Gonzalo called, as they neared him. The men did not break their own conversation. He waved to them as though in pleasant greeting.

"Excuse me," he said again. "Do you not understand? You can't speak that language." He didn't know how to get the men's attention. He waved again, vigorously.

"*Estimado señor*," Gonzalo finally screamed.

One man looked at Gonzalo, and in Spanish said to the blank skin between Gonzalo's two eyes, "I'll speak whatever goddamned language I want," then continued walking straight ahead. Gonzalo had to turn around, to run stupidly after him, yelling out, "I am a Civil Guardsman," which almost made him laugh out loud himself. But then the bird of laughter fell back into his stomach and sunk. He grabbed the man by the shoulder, but now he struggled to lift his tongue. "Your language is illegal," he forced out.

"*Ez zait axola*," the man spat back at Gonzalo. And just as Gonzalo was on the verge of protesting, the man reached his hand into Gonzalo's mouth and filled it with his fingers. Everyone went still. The two men stared at each other. Gonzalo felt his lungs spasm deep in his chest. His eyes began to roll like marbles in their sockets, shedding tears.

When the man removed his hand, he and his group continued past Gonzalo, down the street. The toddler with the small dog had circled back to watch the incident, and the dog's scattered high-pitched barks synced almost seamlessly with Gonzalo's jagged breath.

45. At 5:15 a.m., find the boy sprawled across the stairs to your apartment, asleep.
46. Notice his bare arms, and return to the apartment for the single sweater that you brought with you in your backpack.
47. Outside, let him lead you to the train station.
48. Purchase two tickets for Saint-Jean-de-Luz, a small fishing town near the border with Spain. When he asks you where you're taking him, tell him, "Big lake," because you cannot remember the French word for sea, and when you feel his timid fingers drop a handful of francs into your pocket, return them.
49. While you wait for the train, perched on the hard plastic seats, remember the word for sea in French diverges from Spanish by a single letter: *mar* changes only to *mer*.

50. Board the train.

51. For a second, be unsure of whether or not to place your arm around his seat. Wonder if instead, you should sit on the other side of the aisle.

52. Sit down next to the boy, and keep your hands on your rod, where it rests between your knees. Try not to watch him mimic you.

53. Ask him how old he is. (Answer: Fourteen. You were right.)

54. Ask him what his parents do. (Answer: His mother is the manager of a small hair salon. His father may be a tailor. He's seen bolts of cloth lying about the apartment. Strangely, he's not sure.)

55. Ask him what he does after school. (Answer: He doesn't have a good response for this. He shrugs. Follow other boys around? Walk home the long way through the city and gather details he later tries to recreate on paper, in the drawings he does most afternoons before his parents come home?)

56. Ask him if he might show you some of his drawings. Be surprised at your own disappointment when he tells you no.

57. Watch the profile of his surly face move into and out of a hard patch of sunlight, keeping time with the motion of the train. Recall your mother mocking you for your own surliness in the Basque she only spoke inside the house: *Esnatu, estatua-mutil hori.*

Across the compound, news of Gonzalo's attempted arrest spread. The entire episode depressed him—he heard himself saying foolishly, "I am a Civil Guardsman" over and over again—but men came up to him all evening to offer him their congratulations. Maybe, he thought, they had seen him lying around in the past week and had taken note of his true spinelessness. Or maybe, when far from the barracks and out on patrol, the men secretly found themselves as timid and spineless as he.

"I'm so proud of you," the burly Ángel whispered to Gonzalo, before giving him a kiss on the side of his head, right where his skin met his hair. They had gotten very drunk. From their table at the back of the mess hall, they looked out onto the patio, and beyond that, to the exposed belly of the night. A pale strip of the past day's light still hung above the marshland. Ángel's spit sunk into Gonzalo's ear.

58. Wonder if you should tell Antoine a little more about yourself. Maybe this will help him open up.

59. Tell him that you're thirty-nine years old.

60. Feel embarrassed.

61. Wave hello to the nun in the corner of the car who looks up when you say this. Hear Antoine snort.

62. Ask Antoine what he draws.

63. Listen as he begins cautiously: "Nothing very good." Then, "I've been trying to get better, but my drawings never come out like the things I'm picturing."

64. Nod once. Don't mess this up: start filing through the possible responses. Don't break your cool. Don't try to make eye contact.

65. While you're still searching, hear, "Birds, mostly. Sometimes people. Crowds jockeying to board the train. A swarm of crows pecking the sidewalk outside

a café. A man at his balcony observing the aftermath of a brawl. On the street below him, a sparrow with a messed-up wing."

66. Strain your ears to hear as he tells you, just above the drone of the train engine, that he makes his drawings when he comes home from school, makes them to completion, and as soon as they are done, puts water to the paper, and watches while his lines blur out completely. Be almost positive that you have heard him correctly when he says that ruining the drawings feels as good as making them.

67. Resist the urge to ask him to explain this.

68. Instead, ask him if he keeps the ruined paper. (Answer: "Yes.")

69. Nod once. Do not fight the listing of the train as it lures you back to sleep.

Gonzalo had stopped lingering in his bed in the mornings. Since his first confident day—also the day that had ended with someone else's fist in his mouth—he had recognized the habit as juvenile. He saw how it set him apart from the rest of the men and he did not let himself do it anymore. Instead, he rose with the rest of the barrack, dressed himself in his uniform, and left the compound on time.

The day after his run-in with the man in town, Gonzalo tried to restart down his practiced path. He found the town's central street, but he dreaded having to patrol again, and after half a block he grew tired. He went into one of the bars, and while he waited at the front counter to order a coffee, he noticed the gradual flight of customers to the back of the room: in its

shadowy corners, he could just make out the newly formed pools
of people pushed up against one another. When his coffee came,
he walked away, and he carried the bar's white ceramic cup with
him.

He could not do his job, that was the truth. He turned off
of the street of bars, and began to wander. He was not capable of
making anyone speak a different language. Each time he came
upon another person, he looked into their eyes but he never spoke
a single word. They passed him more and more easily. Pieces of
Basque began to clip his ears. He intentionally lost himself: his
daily walks soon devolved into a willing submission to the labyr-
inth of identical streets, end-marked by identical street corners.

70. Wake up. In your brain, prepare more conversation topics.

71. Prepare your fishing lesson.

72. Three hours have already passed. Wonder if Antoine
    will ask why you had to submit yourselves to a train ride
    that eats up half the day when there's so much coast
    closer to Paris. That coast you could have reached in two
    hours, who knows—maybe less.

73. Wonder if he will ask you how you know your way
    around Saint-Jean-de-Luz and wonder how much to
    tell him about the dozens of visits that you've made in
    recent years. Resolve not to mention anything about
    the life you would resume were you to cross the border
    back into Spain, only 14 km to the west. Instead, tell
    him about the trip you took with your friends when you
    were all eighteen, and so desperately young. How you'd
    gotten very drunk on cheap French wine poured with
    abandon by the waitress making a pass at Iban. How

you all had somehow made it to the tent you'd pitched on the edge of town. There were five of you. How you'd fought with Peio about who was allowed to sleep beside the only girl: Sofía.

As he wandered, some portions of the town, unfortunately, retained a blueprint in Gonzalo's mind. The wan marble of the intact *ayuntamiento*, for example, could not be passed off as the facade of any other building. Nor could he become totally, blissfully, lost in the upper streets, whose height betrayed which way was which. On the few occasions that he managed to remove the sensation of a change in altitude from his step, he caught in his field of view a clue that dismantled the whole charade: a tree, leaning precariously away from him, to mark a decline. A beam of water running persistently in his direction to indicate that he was going up.

74. In your head, calculate just over an hour until you arrive in Saint-Jean-de-Luz.
75. Watch the countryside molt away its unfamiliarity and watch the abundant hills of almost-home roll toward you.
76. Watch the countryside so fervently you do not notice the man who sits down a few rows ahead of you on the train. Do not see him until Antoine nudges you, then take it in: the nondescript clothing, the ski mask that he wears beneath his black beret.
77. Try hard not to stare at the material that obscures and eradicates his face. All that's left are human lips, and through those two narrow slits, a pair of eyes.
78. Do not peer into his eyes—what if he recognizes you?

79. Force your heart rate down to the slap of the train. *You have never worn a ski mask. You don't know this man. He will not recognize you.*

80. In case he does, make a plan: there is a red emergency lever on the window four seats to your left, or the seats themselves might resist the blow of bullets, if it comes to that. Consider crawling beneath them to the door at the far end of the train. Consider starting now.

81. Feel Antoine's head press itself into the space between your skull and your shoulders. Feel the flexible flesh of his nose bend into the side of your neck. Put your arm around him, and register that his body has seized up completely. Even the skin above the muscle: brittle. Like glass.

82. From your brain, delete the whole process of how to construct a bomb. Dismantle it, step by step.

83. Even after the man has gotten off the train, do not move.

84. Do not move even as the hills unravel themselves before you.

85. In another hour, get off the train at Saint-Jean-de-Luz.

. . .

86. Ten years later, at a bar in Guernica, recall the details of that unsettling encounter when a fellow ex-*etarra* recounts ETA's most recent attack: *Etakide-talde batek atsedenaldian zenbiltzan bi polizia espainiar erail zituen Hendaian.*

(In the stretch of days that passed since his total submission to the town, Gonzalo's initial coffee break developed into a daily habit, and it now swallowed up huge swathes of his morning patrol. During those weeks Gonzalo took up the practice of turning off other people's voices when in a bar, or any public meeting place: he dreaded the pressure of assigning a language to sound. He had so honed his ability to shut down his ears that he felt taken aback, nearly violated, when, in the back of a café at the far end of the street of bars, this full sentence of Basque assailed his brain.

His break on that particular morning was barely in its infant stages when he overheard the speaker continue that yesterday, a group of *etarras* had murdered two off-duty Spanish policemen near Saint-Jean-de-Luz. He pictured the men from his mind collecting their guns from the ground and crossing the border. And he knew that he could no longer pretend to be totally, helplessly, deaf to Basque. He buckled with a strange sense of guilt.

Yes, it was news of the border crossing that did it for poor Castilian Gonzalo. He watched his own imaginary ETA fighters disperse, boarding trains in all directions, and he felt—as the days unwound themselves within the dark wooden caverns of local bars, and his Civil Guardsmen pants creased from the infinite hours spent sitting, and it became clear that in the whole length of his time in Guernica, he would never once do his job—that he was, certainly, and without a prayer, trapped in a moving train with them.)

RECUERDOS: EA

The beach in Ea is like a failed word, the sand a long and narrow stroke upon the page, long enough to forget the thing is a beach—it may be something else, a racetrack, a long jumper's pit, a desert in distant land—until what was once negative space turns positive: the water. Infinite, disconcertingly serene. And now, dangling at the mercy of your own buoyancy, it should be clear that wherever you thought that stretch of land had been delivering you, really, it was here:

RECUERDOS: LEMOA

For a long time, visitors to Lemoa found the town nearly impossible to navigate. They came with the knowledge we all acquire in primary school—which arrows on the compass indicate which cardinal direction—but when they reached Lemoa and asked how to get to the nearest café, and the people in Lemoa answered, *It's west of the factory and east of the convent and you can find it two blocks past the central plaza*, nobody from outside of Lemoa, despite knowing the words "factory," "convent," "plaza," "blocks," and "café," could find it in the end.

They didn't see what was easy to see, that when someone says *west of the factory* and *east of the convent*, they really mean *imagine your primary school compass*: draw a line between northwest and southeast, have it start at the mouth of the plaza, and follow that diagonal line two blocks until you've reached the dim, flickering neon sign that says Bar Eder. Order a *cortado*.

To be clear: Lemoa was a town bastioned by two beloved

institutions, a town winged by twin buildings, a town anchored by them, stuck in its place, fixed in its ways the way it was fixed in the ground.

It was natural, in Lemoa, to worship the convent. I'm tempted to say that it would be natural anywhere to worship the place where people worshiped, to love the place where they, in their measured manner, practiced a sort of love. But Lemoa was also an old-fashioned town, full of old-fashioned people, and the convent, to people like us, was a beautiful idea. The whisk of the women's habits, for decades, stirred hearts. The sound of the convent's bells resonated exquisitely with the passage of blood through the veins. Don't be alarmed; when you love someone, you too will notice how these things affect you.

But as much as we cared about the important parts—the prayers, their chasteness, the swell of their skirts—we were shallow people. The convent building embarrassed us: that old, abandoned paper mill bore no markings of saintliness. Though we loved the sisters, it pained us to see them slip between those double doors on which they had painted, in fading gold, a free-hand version of their order's crest. We hated to imagine them down on their knees, pressing their foreheads to those splintering floors—the simple lives they lived behind that clouded glass.

When the cement factory arrived, and the silos for storing cement rose up above us like a chorus of ancient spires, we were relieved. Two warehouses buttressed the compound and the intricate piping of the factory's drainage system wound around the buildings as though a wreath of silver pilasters. When the sun hung at the correct angle to redouble these lines in a multitude of shadows, all their grandeur magnified before our eyes. We spent our lives aware of the factory looming in the southeastern corner of our town—no matter where you stood, you were bound to catch it in your periphery—and we felt grateful for its presence. And, if I'm being honest, greedy, for the way it reminded us of our own smallness.

Eventually, a group of punks memorialized the factory the way we saw it: they snuck through the fence at night and painted on the building the facade of a church. If they were trying to be unruly or subversive or cool their plan fell through; we all joined them.

For a while, in Lemoa, when things were less confusing, "the factory" replaced "north," and "the convent" replaced "south," and whatever inventive directions someone gave you were inevitably based in some way on that rule. But with our factory masquerading as holy and our convent shrouded in disarray, even Mari-Carmen Urribe, whose family has lived in Lemoa for six generations, might falter and forget the difference between the two. Finding little else to guide her, as her points of reference she might anxiously name the fishmongers, or the kitchen supply store, or the trashcans clustered too close together in the park, or the swimming pool. When asked for directions next time, she might stutter and excuse herself entirely, saying that she needs a moment to rest her mind. And then she might go and pray for herself in the privacy of her own home.

FLOCK

I.

From a dell, just outside of town, rose the apartment building
where Miren and her mother lived. Skinny and pale pink. Like a
tongue on the verge of speaking its own apology. Each day after
school, Miren passed through the town's empty municipal lot,
crossed the planked-over stream, and returned to the building. It
embarrassed her for how its height and shoddy exterior diverged
from the uniform town center, which her mother often described
as "tasteful," sometimes with contempt. But as she neared the
building, and it grew gradually larger in the face of the mountain behind it, she often thought that if she had to be a building
herself, maybe it would be this one: tall, but only by illusion. Just
a little bit pink. Strange in a way that made her uncomfortable.

Being thinner than the average building, it was composed of
one apartment per floor, and so from half of the rooms one could
stand at the window and loom over the town beneath them. From

the other half, one could pretend that the town did not exist. It was on that side of the apartment building that Miren tended to linger, and it was there, haunting those rooms one day after school, that she first noticed the women. There were just four of them then. Miren only understood they were shepherding when they finally returned with a herd in tow after four sheepless passes by her apartment. They moved slowly, without any sense of urgency, and without, Miren later noted, a sheepdog.

When the women appeared she could never focus on whatever schoolwork she had half-heartedly been doing. Sometimes it was the sheep she spotted first instead, drifting like a single low-hanging cloud over the mountain.

Though the original sightings occurred from the living room, the bathroom, with its door that shut and locked, offered greater privacy. She was unsure how she found herself, on so many occasions, standing atop the toilet, neck bent at a severe angle, watching.

Miren leaned against the loading docks behind her town's recreational center as her classmates left the building. The dark outlines of their bodies were bridged at the elbows. Her mother had allowed her to walk home from the dance only because she'd be with Patri, who'd planned to sleep over, but Patri had disappeared into the crowd as soon as they'd arrived. Already Miren felt her mother's sorry eyes on her. Already she saw her mother, in her white nightgown, helplessly drawn to the light of Miren's bedroom like a confused and sympathetic moth.

She'd been so occupied with feeling sorry for herself that she missed Jon entirely as he came around the corner. Only after he had repeated Miren's name many times did she hear it.

"Excuse me, *monsieur*," Jon said. "Are you waiting for your parents?"

It's true, they were in the same French class, she'd forgotten that. Miren waited for him to correct himself, but he showed no promise of speaking again and had pronounced the word with such care for its delicate consonants that she answered honestly: "No, a friend." Then she added, "But she might never come."

"*Supér*," he said.

A giggle escaped her, automatic, like a cough.

Clumsily they waded into conversation, forging ahead in the face of discomfort until they arrived at the mundane admissions that feel so intimate when first spoken aloud: *I've never told anyone I love the smell of mothballs on sheets. Sometimes I daydream about sleeping on water.*

Over the course of their conversation, the events that seemed so inevitable to Miren shifted. No longer did the future hold her mother's discovery of her crying alone beneath the bedroom's overhead light, but rather, the three months following that night during which she would date Jon, someone she'd always known existed, but had never spoken to in her life. Of course, once they'd trod into admissions, she didn't mention anything to Jon about the sheep, or the women who followed them. They were barely on her mind. Just wandering the periphery of it, the tip of a hoof only occasionally protruding into her consciousness.

In time, like all couples, she and Jon shrugged off the last remaining scraps of self-consciousness. Hands wandered into new territories, startling both the giver and receiver of the touch. Their parting ritual expanded with this newfound confidence, until it stretched on interminably, often as the day cooly extinguished itself, obscuring Miren's view from the bathroom window. And so whenever she could, she would push Jon out of the house at the peak of the afternoon, back across town, and rush through each stage of the ritual to save half an hour, fifteen minutes, anything, to watch out for the sheep.

Eventually it happened: Jon, after walking her home, held her for the usual stretch, and the women passed by right in front of her, while she was bound up in his arms.

A few weeks later, Miren and Jon were up in his father's tractor. She was sitting on his lap, facing him, when she caught a glimpse of a strange movement in the far corner of the field: the women, one by one, emerged from the trees. To spy them so far from her house was unnerving. She couldn't quite put her finger on the root of that odd sensation that instead of her observing the women, someone had in fact been observing *her*.

That was when she noticed a new figure straggling at the back of the group. They were smaller than the rest, and draped over their slight frame was the blue knit sweater that her mother had made her a few years ago.

Jon nudged her with his nose, but she turned away. "No," she said. She put one foot on the ground to get a better view. "I'm busy." She watched the figure shift their weight in tandem with her, took in their awkward stance, familiar brown hair. It was Miren, out there, staring back at herself.

And then she was gone, replaced by one of the usual women who she recognized from the bathroom window. When Jon had asked her *busy with what*, she ignored him. Only once the women filed back into the forest and disappeared completely did she answer, "I'm just checking the clouds . . . for rain . . ."

❧

When Miren and her mother had dinner alone in their quiet apartment, she stole glances at her mother's face. When her mother ate fish, she often left the bones of bacalao sitting between her lips throughout the meal, as though she were recomposing its spine in her mouth. How could be she be fascinated by these other women when her own mother made her cringe?

A few weeks later, after a town-wide funeral for Benito Zubero, who'd surprised them all with his sudden death, Miren slipped off her shapeless black dress beneath the overhead light of her bedroom, and caught sight of her own reflection in the darkened window. Her mother had told her that Benito had died of bone disease, and she thought of this as she observed her ribcage, barely concealed by flesh. She was like the building: frail. Strange. It was *she* who made people uncomfortable.

That was it, she was sure. She made people uncomfortable. Why else had Patri left her? And was Jon not plotting their separation too? Though she had been convinced that *she* was tiring of *him*, perhaps it was the other way around, and he'd in fact been hoping to bring about her departure since he rounded the corner on her after the school dance.

And her mother. Miren turned off the overhead light so as not to accidentally summon her. The sounds of the TV leaked in from the other room. She'd begun to sense in her mother a new trepidation around her. It made Miren feel dangerous, as though one thoughtless word or gesture had the potential to destabilize the whole house. And in any case, wasn't that face that her mother so often gave her—that expression of wordless sympathy—simply a confirmation of her unease?

On the sidelines of the town's trampled field, Miren watched Jon play a game of pickup soccer while she kept a tally of the goals he himself scored. Her count, however, was nearly identical to the score—he was really, boringly, good—and so it wasn't her fault, who could blame her, when her eyes drifted beyond the gangly boys threading the field, past their netless goalposts, to the trees beyond town. The sun was just above those trees. It slung their shadows over the ground; its rays sleighed into her eyes. In that brief period, when things seemed momentarily fake—everything before the sun flattened to nothing—she spotted the women treading the edge of the forest. Behind them Edurne Zubero, Benito's widow, walked ahead of her own flock of sheep, ushering them into the shadows in twos and threes.

Jon scored another goal and ran a lap around the field, arms raised like a flightless bird. If she squinted and blocked out the sun with her hand, she could see the sheep, but just barely. As though they had joined someplace murky. One of the women waited alongside Edurne, who moved her hand as though she were counting the flock. Four, seven, nine, eleven, thirteen, fifteen, eighteen—Miren looked back to the field; she'd lost the score.

After the game, Jon walked her home. Sweaty, mottled up to knees with mud, he recapped each of the goals:

"Did you get five?

"There were seven total."

"But five for me, right?"

"Something like that."

"*Oye*, you're being coy, I saw you counting." He swooped in to kiss her on the cheek, but then suddenly embarrassed, he pulled back and looked toward the field, now submerged in shadow.

She'd squeezed his hand, touched faintly by affection for him. But when they arrived at her building, the sun having set and the clear sky dimming fast, he embraced her for so long that she wanted to cry. Andoni, her downstairs neighbor, passed them, and held the door to the building for Miren, but, when met with a blank stare, he let it fall behind him. As Jon rocked her back and forth, she did what she could to hold in her tears. Once Jon finally released to her apartment, she went directly to her room. She'd long resolved not to waste her time looking out for the women after dark.

And she wasn't *actually* looking, several nights later, when they passed. She was using the toilet rather than standing atop it, but through the open bathroom window she heard each footstep distinctly. "Your laces are whacking the ground," someone said. "I don't care if they're not bothering you, they're bothering *me*."

By the time she ran out of the building, the women were already crossing the planked-over stream. She did not expect herself to call out to them, and she certainly didn't expect them to turn around. But she called, and they turned, and they waited for her there as she approached.

Up close, she was taken aback to find their faces complicated by networks of lines that clouded her understanding of their features. She felt, for the first time in her life, embarrassed to be young.

"I'd like to learn how to shepherd," she managed. When none of them said anything, she attempted again: "Really. Sincerely. I'm interested in tending sheep."

A gray-haired woman stepped forward, her face projecting a strange, opaque smile. Abruptly, Miren added, "I have noticed that none of you have husbands."

"Or at least," she said, "it really seems like you don't have husbands. Since you're always together . . . walking."

One of the women coughed, out of boredom possibly, or offense.

Miren sped up. "And I live here." She flung her arm in the direction of her building. "And I've seen you pass by, almost every day."

These last few words escaped the trial of her brain completely: "Recently, my boyfriend left me." She repeated it another time to remind herself that this was now the truth. A moment ago she'd decided on this: "He left me." A weightlessness consumed her, so forceful that it wrenched her up out of her body. From that other place, that place of no gravity, where it seemed dangerously possible that an arm or a hand might separate and float away, she said it: "Please, let me join you."

II.

The women slept in the woods.

The sheep spent each day grazing in the hills behind their town, and, after following the sound of their distant bells for hours, the women, at night, reclaimed them. Afterward, they arranged a layer of blankets on the ground and slept right there, beside the herd.

When they reconvened with the sheep that first night, Edurne pointed to one and said, "This guy I call my Benito." She slapped his flank but he paid her no attention. "He's ignoring me now, I guess we're in some kind of fight." The sheep's ear looked like it had been chewed up in a brawl, or by some roaming wild boar. Dried blood was caked over the stump. When Miren dared herself to ask what had happened to Benito—she didn't think to clarify, to the sheep or to the husband—Edurne answered without pause that he'd been kidnapped by a group of *etarras* on his way home from work. She was told that he'd been tortured; she had no idea how much. It would be a mischaracterization, by some measure a slander, to say that Edurne laughed as she said it, but it occurred to Miren with a bit of horror that Edurne had in fact seemed open to laughter, eager to admit the absurdity of the situation if only someone provoked her.

Before they went to sleep, the women set up their camp and boiled a communal pot of beans. Beside them, the sheep were allowed to graze as they pleased. Almost immediately, they resumed the process of losing themselves.

"It's totally possible that they cut off his ear," Edurne said with no warning, the next day, when she and Miren were side by side. Nobody had had an extra sweater to offer Miren, so she'd done as another woman instructed: she'd tied a blanket around her shoulders for warmth. All morning she felt ashamed of it, conscious of how the other women must have seen her.

Edurne continued, "Xabi, you know which one—the baker—makes note of every piece of news that passes through the shop." Edurne's face contorted itself into her expression from the day before, that grimace which disguised a secret pleasure. "And apparently, that gives him license to wreak havoc on the rest of us. Whenever I go in to buy bread he won't let me leave without telling me gruesome details. He doesn't discriminate— people tortured by ETA, *etarras* by the Civil Guard—it doesn't matter to him. He has a thing for violence, that man. . . . Imagine that," she said. "A severed ear, every time you need a baguette."

Miren started, and Edurne, recovering herself, rearranged her face into a deliberate softness. "Don't worry," she said. "I won't repeat what he's told me."

Despite all of Xabi's information, she hadn't learned what

happened to her husband between the moment he was kidnapped and when his body arrived in a shipping container at the foot of the town church. Father Mendoza had discovered Benito early that morning, and had him transferred immediately to a coffin, the lid of which was never, after that, lifted. Edurne had no idea whether he was missing an ear or anything else; the last chapter of her husband's life she'd filled in with her own awful imagination.

After dinner the second night, avoiding the topic of Benito, Edurne recounted to Miren a story about a cousin of hers whom she'd always liked until she hadn't anymore. Miren lay on her back, listening.

When nighttime came to the forest, the trees descended over them, their branches black against the field of clouds charged with old, expired light. Miren stared at the sky until it confused her and she had to close her eyes. Each night, wrapped in someone else's blanket and conscious of a dozing body on either side of her, Miren was seized by the sensation of lying beside her mother, and, at the same time, beside Jon. She imagined rolling over to discover her head in the chest of someone familiar. In these experiments it was either of them, both of them, every time.

III.

If this were a fable, Miren would have begged the women to deposit her at the edge of town and, from there, would have burst into the apartment and convinced her mother to join the female shepherds with her, thrusting these few salvaged details before her as glittering proof: the thick skin of life could be pulled back. The world these women made in the woods offered an idea of what lay beneath: a tenderness, a miraculous tolerance for being bruised.

But for however young those women made her feel, Miren was certainly not a child—fables, with their neatness, their awful circularity, had long bored her. In the books that she read for school, she'd several times had the instinct to cut pages and replace them with fragments of the news: *The boy was discovered in good spirits, but faced insurmountable medical hurdles. The End.*

And, if she were honest, the details of her brief time with the women did not glitter before her like some reward.

Ever since Edurne had mentioned it, the thought had run through her mind like a blade: Benito, who owned the metalworks factory, kidnapped by ETA.

And though it wasn't his fault—of course it wasn't—Benito became the route through which a dark and formless threat infiltrated her. While she had never before associated him with the things that frightened her, now, no matter how she tried, she could not cleave him from them: the conmen meat vendors from the South who dominated the market with their awful bravado and expired *jamón*. The bottom of the ravine with its shrieking river, or the stream that passed before her house. She couldn't resist the thought that he'd placed that splintering plank there himself.

On the third day, she was fantasizing about her escape when the sheep ambushed them in the middle of the afternoon. A jangle of distant bells grew quickly louder, and then the entire shuddering flock streamed through the trees. In an instant, the forest became glutted with white. Edurne, next to Miren, was carried several paces away by the mass. Even after the initial swell subsided, the sheep needled their way in between the women, separating them from one another.

Once the commotion subsided, someone pointed out the distant bleats sounding from down the hill: a few confused sheep had gotten separated from the herd. Miren volunteered to collect them without hesitation.

Down there, as she darted from rock to rock, the world acquired a new cleanness. The women's voices fell away behind her. Though she'd not yet settled on any opinion about them—she could not say whether she loved the women, or felt love's inverse—she had no doubts that, in that moment, she was leaving them.

No, she knew she would not burst through the doors of her mother's apartment, pull the onion out from under her knife as she prepared a *marmitako*, or perhaps a *pisto*. She wouldn't announce to her mother that to be a single woman was a terrible, lonely business. That the sight of their two nightgowns drying alone on the clothesline caused her undue pain. And she would not, as she had once fantasized about doing, pick out the tallest umbrella from the stand in their hallway, and thrust it into her mother's hand for use as a walking stick.

She would not make her mother join the women—she had no doubts about it. Nor would she stay with them either, condemning herself to an endless search for roving sheep. And this was, ultimately, why she was walking along the side of the road, back in the direction of their town, when Leire Ugarte's mother drove past.

The car slowed to a stop just before her. As Leire's mother got out of the vehicle, she released a string of curse words that came to a head in "*¿Mi hija, qué bárbaro es esto?*"

"*Dios bendito*," she said to herself. She stood before Miren, inspecting her wrinkled dress and the scuff marks on her legs. "*Alguien te ha hecho daño chica*." Someone has done you harm.

"Hi, Conchi, I'm okay," she said. "Just talking a walk."

Leire's mother barked some unintelligible noise, and slapped Miren on the arm. "Listen to you! Only wild boar go walking here." She looked around, as though expecting one of the other town mothers to climb out of the trees to corroborate her point.

Leire got out of the car. Miren recognized her from the group of girls Patri had joined. She nodded at Miren, who smiled so halfheartedly that only one corner of her mouth turned upward, like she'd flinched instead, or sneezed.

"*Pobrecita*." Leire's mother took a step toward her, and placed one finger beneath Miren's chin. She wore a silk shirt printed with leopard spots. Through it, Miren could see the outline of her bra. The pattern made a strange contrast with the real forest behind her. Leire's mother said, "Get in my car."

And, again, because this wasn't a fable—this was her life—there was no question that Miren would submit without protest and ride silently in the backseat all the way to their own town, conscious, the entire drive, of Leire looking disinterested in the seat before her. She made an effort not to look into the car's right-side mirror, on the off chance their gazes would meet.

As the unfamiliar mountains buckled to signs she was entering her own terrain, she found it impossible to tell if these sights produced the warmth of recognition or whether they came to her simply as a series of forms she was conscious of having seen before. The hunters' bars, Geltoki and Gure Lur. The cluster of shanty farms on the edge of Bergara. Their corrugated metal roofs and plastic irrigation tubs. The road turned to a bridge and the car cruised over a gaping ravine. Finally, they skirted the periphery of her town and arrived in the municipal lot, beside the sad, planked-over stream.

As they neared, Leire's mother lit a cigarette and Leire pulled one out of the pack as soon as her mother had put it down between them.

"Take it if you want," Leire's mother said, without looking at her daughter. "But just like your Aunt Mari, you'll go young." Then, from guilt, or else from the desire to lay the conversation to rest in some other way, she'd looked into the rearview and said, "Look at that, your dad keeps forgetting that silly hat in the car."

As Miren watched the car pull out of the lot, the sight of the two cigarettes dangling from either window sent a spasm of affection through her. She had insisted to Leire's mother there was no need to accompany her into the apartment. There existed no explanation, in any case, that *she* could give for Miren's disappearance.

In some other, different kind of fable, perhaps her own mother never would have realized she'd been missing. Or better—the building would be gone, and she'd find herself walking in the opposite direction, toward town, where she lived now. It felt like a cruel reminder of her reality that those days with the women ended like this: Miren nearing the building, trying her best to look through it to the clear, naked sky, as she imagined her mother's face on the other side of the door and considered the many possible ways she might apologize.

IV.

But then, if it's truly unpleasant to leave things that way, perhaps it would be no less honest to end elsewhere. For instance, earlier, after she'd left the women in the woods—

Through the trees, she'd descended into an unfamiliar town, where the distant jangle of bells led her along a series of winding streets to the foot of an enormous, professional soccer stadium. Her few missing sheep lingered on a patch of grass beside its front door.

Those were blissful hours, the few, who knows how many, she spent perched on the stadium's bleachers. When she'd wandered inside, the sheep had followed her instinctively, and now they grazed idly on the field below. She'd done it—she'd left the women—and in the delirium of her relief, she lost all clarity of vision: the sheep, the goalposts, the sidelines devolved into a jumble of white and green shapes. The tide of her former life tugged on her, but she would not, at least for a little while, turn herself over to it.

Perhaps she and Jon would come to see a game, she'd been thinking, when a mob of boys burst onto the field. It seemed an illusion, or a practical joke: from her unfocused eyes, twenty, possibly even thirty clones of Jon materialized all at once.

There were shrieks and "*joder*" coming from all corners of the stadium. After a few moments of chaos, someone screamed "*Oye, chicos*—is someone going to get these fucking animals off of the field? *Este hijo de puta* Pedro promised me he was going to practice his penalty kicks today, isn't that right?" There was a pause. "*¿Eh? ¿Qué dices Pedrito?*"

She slid off her seat so she was no longer visible from the field below. Lying on the concrete floor of the stadium seating, she listened to the chaos the sheep incited. And because, thank goodness, their bells rang like crazy in the middle of it all, she remained barely perceptible, blissfully anonymous, when, for the first time in months, she began to laugh.

V.

Though actually, if one were willing to wait a bit longer to see it put down on paper, Miren herself would prefer to end with this: her first migraine, age sixteen, at the market in Durango. A hole formed in the corner of her vision, and as soon as Miren mentioned it, her mother led her by the hand through the maze of stalls, the lettuce heads and stray peppers that littered the ground disappearing into the hole as she moved.

Little more than three years had passed since Miren's time with the women in the forest, though now she could remember almost none of it. Aside from a few random details, the period became irretrievable as soon as it ended. But like that hole in her vision, she was aware of those few days perching there in the corner of her consciousness. When she tried to look at them directly, they yielded nothing. An absence; the outline of a memory.

In truth, it wasn't until many migraines later, when she was already an adult, that she awoke to the similarity between those two sensations. On that first occasion, Miren followed her mother blindly to a seat in a quiet corner of the regional train station, where her mother directed her to put her chest to her knees, and to close her eyes. Her mother then knelt down before her and took Miren's head between her own two hands.

"*Amatxu*, it's awful." Miren's voice broke. "*Ama*," she croaked. "I've never felt like this before." Nausea knocked at the back door of her throat. Even with her eyes closed, the sinkhole in her vision remained. Round. Soft edges. Nearly the shape of a cloud, or a sheep . . . though a shape like that could have been any animal. Anything.

RECUERDOS: BERMEO

In Bermeo, there are a lot of places where you might put your-self to sleep. The most mundane option, which first must be addressed, is in your own bed, atop your own mattress, in the narrow bedroom inside your own apartment. But there are a whole cascade of other places where you might consider putting your aching body to rest, and those too deserve attention.

On the bench in the park that tops the cliff behind the town, you might place yourself, and let the wind that scrapes off the sea whip at your exposed side. Though it feels like it might lift you up—like it might gather you in its phantom arms and cast you out dangerously over the water—know that it will not.

There are stairways that you might also try, if you have begun with the park above the town but for whatever reason it is not the right resting place for you. From the park, you might follow a path that cuffs the side of the cliff, and that will deliver you gently down to the port. Mid-descent, if the feeling takes you, and if the tilt of the path seems conducive to sleep, you might lay yourself flat against the stone walkway, and aim to fit your head into a rut in the cobblestones. Find the place, I would say, where the four corners of four different stones meet. Try it; rest your head there.

If you do end up getting all the way to the port, and the slope of the path has not distracted you on your way, down there you'll find the staircases where I have always dreamed of sleeping. You might set yourself at the top of one of those staircases, the ones that emerge like veins from the hillside, almost hidden between the tall, thin portside houses. Up there, on the highest landing, where the staircase meets the stone face of the cliff, you might curl yourself into the space between two buildings, and rest unnoticed by anyone except for the surly older women who climb those steps to their front doors. If you're lucky, they'll see your body and leave atop you the fishing net they spent the day painstakingly repairing, and though you'll probably feel punctured by their gruffness, you might feel grateful for the pleasant weight of those nets, and the way they filter out the cold like they filter out fish. From the top landing, you should be able to see a narrow streak of the horizon. Like a swathe of paint going up a page, it will shyly assert itself between the encroaching walls of the buildings on either side. While it seems that they grow closer together each year, know that they do not.

Of course, I'm ignoring where I've wanted to sleep for all of time, but that's because it's embarrassing to say. The truth is there would be no better place to sleep in Bermeo than sprawled atop the mild water that cradles the boats moored in the harbor.

But enough lusting after the impossible.

Inside the portside church, you might put your back to a

wooden pew and try your hand at sleeping beneath the Virgin's crude unblinking eyes. The bench, after all, is sure to be more comfortable than where her withered wooden body rests, suspended three-quarters of the way up the wall from posts attached at her hips and neck. When putting yourself to sleep, you cannot forget the greater portion of an hour you might spend praying that her body is as lifeless and unfeeling as it appears. You cannot forget that in the sanctuary of the church, all your simple thoughts are reborn prayers.

RECUERDOS: SANTUTXU

From Santutxu, the rest of the city appears on a tilt. The flat central boulevards appear off-kilter, and the Nervión, the river that weaves through the valley, looks planted in the earth at an angle. The shrunken people seem to move as though one leg were longer than the other. But the residents of Santutxu, up on that mountain, know that it is *they* that exist on a slant. As they look down at the planar expanse of the city center, they have (yes, and here I am firm about saying they *all* have) the urge to spit and watch it skid down the hill into the flat, elegant plazas below.

Santutxean butchers—more than the butchers of Basurto, Barakaldo, Las Arenas, or Indautxu—struggle with the distinct problem of slipping meat inside their display cases. Some have built contraptions out of old shipping crates to rig the angle of the case away from the protective glass, and some have created a barrier—an impediment to keep the girth of their ham and liver slabs in place—but in all cases the reality of their crooked neighborhood is that the angle of the mountain can never be sufficiently offset; the thick pink hunks never cease to drift, at an average pace of three centimeters an hour, down to that glass. If you stopped by at, say, seven in the afternoon; you would find the bricks of meat at their final resting place, their veined insides splayed and flat against the pane. And you might press your own flesh against the pane—in your case, the storefront window—to feel the contortion of blood vessels that must also be present in the meat. And you might, through the stacked Santutxean apartment buildings, watch the sun slip down the hill to the Gran Vía.

Santutxean dreams suffer a similar tilt effect. Santutxean children, accustomed to living at an angle, when they imagine the physical location of their dreams, imagine them not suspended in a cloud above their heads but rather pooled in the most downhill corner of their bedroom. As though the cloud had once existed, yes, until it accumulated too much dream material, and it too became a victim of Santutxean gravity.

And in the art rooms inside the primary schools these children attend, the paintings stowed in the drying racks are forever at risk of becoming a puddled mess. If the paint for whatever reason is left too watery, those poor portraits—so labored over—are doomed to dissolve. Pools will collect where the paint is still loose and, on that Santutxean slant, catch a current of motion and begin to bleed. The thick stroke meant to indicate a forehead will send its excess paint straight into the painted child's eyes. A nose will become filled with errant brown or green. The children might take these paintings home to their parents, and say to them, *Here is a portrait of my other self.*

❨

Behind the sparse, white-tiled bars suspended on that hill, the barroom trash piles up inside of the trash bins. In the hours before the trash collector comes around, the napkins, bottles, cans, and eggshells overflow their receptacles, casting their briny smell over the street. The tuna cans, in particular, are liable to escape when the pile, grown too large, buckles under the weight of the trash bin's hinged cover. The cans roll out from their place at the top of the heap, and escape, their silver spherical bodies spinning down to the city. There is a dead end, a little abandoned street in the old district, where the fallen cans collect. But no trash collector from either neighborhood has ever thought to look there.

I have lived in Santutxu, and so all of these things I know to be true. And I haven't yet added that the tarts in Santutxu, if you happen to have a kitchen also betrayed by the tilt, tap up against the oven door within minutes of being put inside. Through the window in your oven, you will see the place where the dough, like the meat—and your cheek—bares its timid flesh against the glass.

CECILIO

The first notes began as Cecilio stripped off the bedding in the children's room. He stopped, sheet still in hand, half-risen from the mattress. The sound of the cello always provoked the same sensation in him: that the melody traveled on the bow, and that the bow, instead of sliding across the neck of the instrument, was moving into and out of his skull. When the music paused, he was alarmed to find himself again in the strange, dated-looking room, the walls papered with yellowed drawings. In the center were two twin beds, pushed together.

The music had come through the window, and now, down in the street, Cecilio wandered hungrily, looking for a performer. It was midday: the wide treeless boulevards were rolling with heat, and nearly empty. Nobody was out strolling for pleasure. Neither were they, like him, combing the neighborhood for a street musician he suspected might not exist.

With each step the music grew fainter, and, bored and

disoriented, he let his attention drift to the windows of the first-floor apartments, where he made eye contact with a girl yanking up her tights. Following this incident, he set his sight higher, to the topmost windows of each building. The angle was so steep that he never saw inhabitants, only the tips of their living room walls where they met the ceiling. That normal crease from this new angle looked so alien, so unintelligible, that he perceived the whole as a single plane, sliced diagonally by some sort of arbitrary line. Arbitrary, too, was the abundance of molding, sconces, and picture frames that littered half the plane, while the other—the ceiling—remained relatively spare . . .

He hadn't always been so attuned to these details—he could barely recall the decorations that cluttered his parents' house. But for the first time he was making his own home, crafting a life out of mismatched furniture, wall clocks, cracked china vases, and figurines—the odd trappings of this apartment they inherited from his wife's family.

There was no graceful place, amidst all of these items, to store their own belongings, in Cecilio's case, his few relics from the war: the leather pouch in which he'd kept his ammunition, the four-pronged fisherman's anchor he'd used to ford the jagged peaks of Mount Saibi, his black beret. Noemí would not want them lying around, he assumed, and whenever he roamed through the city, entering storefronts at random to plead for a job, neither was anyone impressed by Cecilio's short stint as a soldier. He didn't even take pride in sharing it, but how else could he explain the wrench thrust into his plans to become a teacher, the fourteen years he spent doing the only thing he had the skills for: plowing his father's middling crops, defending them from grazing deer, warding off frost, malnourished thieves?

Back in the apartment, he dragged the sack of this equipment into the children's room, where behind that closed door it would hopefully be forgotten. As soon as he went in, however, he was met again with the lilt of the cello. He dropped the equipment and cut directly over to the window.

Immediately before him was the back of another building. On either side of it were the backs of two more buildings, which, together with his own, created an enclosed space. Though from this high up, it more resembled a hole. At the bottom was a tiled courtyard. *Why a courtyard*, Cecilio thought, *when there was no discernible way to enter or leave that space?* He had never lived in an apartment building before, and so he wasn't sure what he'd expected, but he felt certain it wasn't this: a strange vertical tunnel streaked with grime, where people hung their drying sheets, where graying underwear fluttered in the breeze, and where sticking your head too far out the window produced the sensation of falling into that terrible chasm between the buildings.

In the chasm, however, the cello resounded. It was almost unreal: crisper than any recording he'd heard, nearer to him than any performer had ever been. And while sound, in the hole, seemed to detach from its origin, over the course of several movements of music, Cecilio became fairly certain that its source was the apartment directly across the way. He tipped his head against the window frame. The sun was mild, too kind, one of those afternoons that feel almost like a dream. Dazedly, he watched the curtains of the opposite apartment breathe. Then the cello stopped abruptly and Cecilio saw the dark outline of a figure rising behind them. He swiftly shut the window and left the room.

That night, Noemí returned home with two water-damaged books from her new job at a library in the old district. An elderly woman was cleaning out her apartment and had donated her entire collection.

"Maybe you don't need a new edition of Galdós, but I thought you wouldn't mind," she said, while Cecilio flipped through the books after dinner. "She must have brought in a hundred books, all of them damaged. I don't know what she thought we could do with them." Cecilio nodded. "She brought them in a little wheeled shopping bag. Like this." She mimed lugging the cart behind her. "She could barely move it."

"You didn't want to say no, I imagine."

"Even after it was emptied," Noemí continued, "I had to help her wheel it over the threshold and carry it down the front steps. God knows how she got it there. In the alley, Cecilio, before she left, she asked me to take a look at her bruises. Just to let her know if they looked serious or not."

"And?"

"Three going up a wrist, and"—she pulled down the collar of her shirt in order to demonstrate—"one on her chest. But large, kind of spread out, like a puddle. And the size of a small bird."

"Well . . . ," Cecilio said, turning a page of the book. "It happens to older people. My mother, too . . ."

"Of course. But what would you have said? I just told her something dumb, to sleep an extra hour at siesta. Then I said, '*Mil disculpas*, I can't leave my desk unattended,' and I ran away."

"If she was emptying her whole apartment, couldn't you have refused them and asked for something else in return?" He thought of the tops of the walls that he'd spotted earlier that day, on his search for the music. "A set of candleholders, what do you think?" He held up a book in either hand. "One for each."

He'd tried to tell her about the cello as they ate, but just as he'd been about to mention it, a piece of potato had fallen from Noemí's fork into her water glass. They'd both broken into giggles, and the rest of the dinner was lost.

By the spring of 1937, when Cecilio had joined the group of Republican soldiers living in the mountains, construction of the concrete bunkers that surrounded the city had more or less stopped. Down in Bilbao, people called them the Ring of Iron, a ridiculous name: confident, nearly boorish, and so ignorant. They had no idea, he assumed, that long stretches, on either end of the ring, were unfinished. Walking past, one could see places where the concrete had not been fully poured and the ribcage of metal reinforcements poked through.

The sight of those bunkers, on the drive up to his post, had frightened him. When he'd seen them, Cecilio had been thankful to be stationed in the interior, toward the center of the ring. Though General Mola's troops were still relatively far off, each of the men in Cecilio's platoon was equipped with a bayonet in case of a premature attack. As soon as he picked it up Cecilio felt ridiculous. The knife stretched out so far in front of him that he had trouble recognizing it as something within his control.

The only other man as inept with the bayonet was Fito, who was more or less the same age as Cecilio, both of them almost, but not quite, twenty-one. On the afternoon they were driven up to the bunker, Cecilio, sitting on the curb in front of the Plaza de la Encarnación, had been immediately intimidated by Fito—his elegant shirt that had clearly been pressed and his easy kindness to the other men. From his pocket Fito pulled out a tin of lemon candies and offered them around. Several times, on the ascent into the dim, low-hanging clouds, the truck hit a bump and Cecilio caught a glance of Fito's face as it jolted into the rearview: his features, stark and thickly drawn, comfortably asserted their own handsomeness. By contrast, Cecilio felt as though he could go either way: attractive to those who liked him, inoffensive and fleeting to the rest.

Because of his appearance, Cecilio expected Fito to be a fantastic soldier. But Fito didn't care about the war. He loved his parents, he told Cecilio, of course he wanted to protect them—that was the only reason he'd allowed himself to get roped into what he called "this whole ridiculous charade." But it was his small act of rebellion that he made no effort to command the bayonet with any grace. Once he'd gone so far as to sabotage both their reputations when he'd dug the tip of its stake into the ground and attempted to rest his elbow on the butt of the gun. It was the sort of pose one performed for a camera, the sort of photograph one mailed to a girlfriend, or a mother. But the bayonet stretched all the way up to Fito's shoulders—there was no way to pose beside it with any ease. Attempting decorum, they'd suppressed their laughter, though they merely retched it out later, in an eruption of hiccups, just as the officer from their squad launched into a speech.

But worse for Fito still was when a commander from another battalion visited their post. At the time, the soldiers' morale was particularly low: whatever inspired the men to join the Republican front, and to be certain, it differed for each, waned over the weeks they wasted inside the bunker. Sleeping on blankets on the ground. Wrapping their heads in scraps of cloth at night so as not to wake up with ears gone numb. Some idiot proposed that, to save time on the cooking, they make rice in enormous batches, so that's what they did—ate leftover rice for weeks, until it poisoned them. To wake in the night and hear some distant vomiting was commonplace.

Despite the state of their platoon, Pérez had arrived, improbably, with a cello. He played the instrument each day for the sergeants at Cecilio's base. At around seven or eight in the afternoon, all the commanders descended on the cluster of looted chairs assembled by the entrance to the bunker.

The music was not intended for the ordinary soldiers, but with Pérez positioned right there—and perhaps this was by design—no one could escape the sound. Many men complained that it continued into their dreams. Whatever privacy they previously enjoyed during sleep was now disturbed by Pérez's sonatas, those jittery, lurching notes like a pair of hands that jostled them in the night just to keep them awake.

Fito too felt the effects of the music: his eyes went hungry as he passed by the circle. After learning that Fito had studied the cello in his childhood, Cecilio once, when they were sent out for firewood, thought he saw Fito cradling a log, assessing its capacity to be made into an instrument. Immediately, however, he felt embarrassed for having rushed to such a sentimental conclusion. Surely that hadn't been on Fito's mind as they'd browsed the trees for rotting trunks, later hacked them into pieces small enough to light.

One evening, as they were filing into the bunker for dinner, Pérez addressed the soldiers for the first time. "Anyone who wants a turn on the instrument can try it," he announced. He looked around at the whole group. "Any one of you—come on! Please, don't anyone be shy." And honestly—he looked kind. There was something charming about the way that, when Pérez smiled, the lines in the corners of his eyes flared out. It gave Cecilio the impression of a curtain being drawn open, revealing, it was natural to assume, a vulnerable man.

Down in the bunker, the soldiers were passing around servings of dinner when they heard Fito take his turn on the cello. He played more slowly, and with more lust for the instrument, than Pérez. For the first time, Cecilio was struck by that sensation: the bow, traveling into and out of his head. But Fito lasted on the cello no more than a few minutes.

Later, when Cecilio was returning his plate, he caught, framed in the doorway at the top of the stairs, a sliver of the following scene: Fito on his knees, Pérez tipping into Fito's mouth the bucket of oil they used for frying meat the rare times a ration was delivered to their camp. Cecilio made it a practice never to look into that bucket when he passed by—congealed globs of fat and other unidentifiable flecks floated around in the oil. It had turned a brownish shade of red from frying last month's chorizo. Through the sporadic dinner conversation, he listened to the sounds of Fito from above: his quiet gags, like howls turned inside out.

Cecilio stood around that stack of dishes, chatting with a few people, killing time. After he felt he'd waited long enough, he crossed in front of the staircase again, but when he'd looked up, the two men were gone. A few minutes later, he noticed Pérez had returned to his usual spot. He sat atop a carved wooden chair, one foot up on a rung. An officer from their platoon passed him a glass of wine.

Once everyone had gone off to sleep, Cecilio went up and

hung around outside the bunker. Back down in the city, he'd bought a packet of tobacco but his rolling papers had gotten ruined, one afternoon, in the rain. Since then, he'd been experimenting with leaves instead. That night, while he waited, he tried to roll a cigarette, but every sound from the forest offered to deliver Fito. Even when Cecilio could get his mind to focus, his fingers remained distracted, barely responsive to his attempts to pinch the tobacco into place. Each one he tried to roll turned out baggy and burned through in a second.

When Fito returned to the bunker, hours later, nothing more than the tap of his feet was discernible in the total darkness. No hint of a body. It was possible to build him from the sounds: boots unlacing, the crackling of joints. Though on many nights leading up to that, the two men had slept beside each other, that night, Cecilio made no effort to stop Fito from settling on the other side of the room. A private groan. A body, lowering itself to the ground.

"Apparently what they have to do is remove the roots," Noemí's mother was saying. "He told me it was 150 pesetas, can you imagine that? I almost don't trust him. My sister's hairdresser has a very good dentist in Amorebieta, apparently."

A cloud of discomfort cohered behind Cecilio's eyes. Then came a burst of little pricks as it developed definite edges: the cry asserting its shape. Since the cello's intrusions into their apartment, certain details of the episode had offered themselves up to him, but the whole memory only came together that afternoon.

"In that case, you've got to call Tía Antonia, no?" asked Noemí. They were at a bar around the corner from her mother's house. She slouched back in the plastic chair. "Ask her to ask her hairdresser how much he charges."

"I called yesterday, but Manolito picked up, so you know what that was like: he had to tell me all the nice things his teacher has said about him this week. He wanted to recite the new psalm he's studied."

"*Dios.*"

"Propaganda," said Noemí's mother, reaching for the bowl of olives. "What can we expect though, his parents are very lazy, they don't correct him . . ." She bit down and made a show of her pain. Cecilio could not stop the tears. A strand of mucus stretched to his chin. He lurched forward for a napkin, and the two of them turned to look at him.

"Pilar," he'd said, bunching up the napkins beneath his nose. "I'm so sorry. I had a very bad toothache last year. So painful." He pushed out his chair and rose from the table while Noemí and her mother watched him with confusion. When he steadied his eyes enough to register their expressions, he mouthed that he was heading to the bathroom, nodded dazedly toward the bar, and then wandered off in the opposite direction, across the plaza.

He walked until he got to a set of stairs that led down to the city center, slipped beneath its metal banister and stretched out on the low concrete wall that bounded the staircase. What was his pride worth anymore, he thought, as he cried there for a few minutes, until he heard the sound of teenage boys approaching and sprang up to evacuate the spot. In the square below, there was nothing but small businesses, most of them shuttered for the afternoon. The only storefront open was a tailor shop, and so he lingered there, beside a naked mannequin, until he unnerved the seamstress with his erratic breathing and was asked to leave.

When Noemí came down the steps, Cecilio was loitering

outside the tailor's in an undershirt. He'd removed his button-down, balled it up, and clutched it to his face. Intermittently, he crumpled into a squat.

With Noemí's help, he rose, and she led him into the building's shadow. There, she gently pried the soaking shirt from his face. Until then, he hadn't noticed that in one hand she carried a Coke in a barroom glass, which she offered to him before setting it on the ground.

He put up no fight when Noemí gathered his face into her shoulder. She stroked the back of his hair as though he were a child. When she asked what upset him, he said limply, "A thing between friends." He added, "It's nothing. From a long time ago." She nodded, and then Cecilio felt her step away. He opened his eyes to Noemí probing for him through the layer of muck he felt drying, as though a mask, over his face.

"Cecilio . . ." She held a hand to his shoulder to steady him. Despite this, she spoke without much warmth: "Please. You're at the beginning of a new period of your life."

By October the cello was playing at all hours of the day. Cecilio would wake to its music and wander through the apartment to stare bewilderedly out at the empty chasm beyond the children's room. The other apartment was, again, so close. He could not look at it without measuring the distance in his mind: no more than two paces, three, through the air, to get across.

And the bow of the cello was still *in* his brain, slicing it down to useless ribbons of tissue. No longer communicating with one another, these separate parts sent their own signals into the void so he was at once zooming down tangents, holding two unlike sensations beside each another, reshuffling his bank of experiences to reveal patterns, and ordering them again. Without any provocation, the memory of Fito began to perfect itself: the tin of candies had been pale green, the circular lid inscribed with block letters—the name of the confectioners. Painted around the perimeter, an ornate blue wreath. In the forest, when they'd been scavenging for firewood, hadn't Cecilio once spotted Pérez through the trees? Hadn't he thought it strange to see him there, had been about to investigate it, when Fito said, "Hey, I don't mean to embarrass you but I've already got double the branches you do, and I don't even care about this shit," before pulling him by the elbow in the opposite direction? And hadn't the wine passed to Pérez when back at the bunker actually been some other, stronger drink?

A few weeks after the incident with Pérez, Cecilio's whole platoon had frantically relocated forty kilometers to the south-east in order to confront General Mola's troops as they advanced. The butt of a bayonet prodded him awake, and alongside the other panicked men he packed his sack, dressed, then stumbled down the mountain to the road, where a row of black cars idled in the dark. Each of the vehicles was painted with a slapdash white cross to look like an ambulance. "Our free pass, brothers," someone remarked as Cecilio slid behind Fito into the backseat. "If, on the road, we meet someone wanting us dead, this lucky idiot can tell them we already are."

He was incapable of suppressing the assault of details, and one morning Cecilio woke in a rage, hurried through the house, and shut and locked all the windows. With the apartment fully sealed, only the strongest, most resonant notes passed through the glass. But they were at the mercy of a cruel autumn heat wave. While the morning passed, bearable and relatively silent, the sun welled up in the apartment and by midafternoon it became uninhabitable. When Noemí arrived home, he'd been reduced to his boxers—though those too he'd sweat through—and he was drunk off a bottle of sweet orange liqueur they'd been given for their wedding.

That night, after Noemí fell asleep, Cecilio felt his way through the dark to the children's room, where he removed the four-pronged anchor from the closet—his crude wartime grappling hook—and scanned the distance between his apartment and the one across the chasm. To the memory of that ceaseless music, he reacquainted himself with the heft of the hook, made sense of its shape with his hands.

His neighbor's window had been left open, and the anchor hit the floor with a dull clang. Cecilio waited to make sure that the sound hadn't roused anyone, and for a few moments the night felt suspended from above, held motionless by some hand. He tugged the rope until the anchor hooked onto the windowsill. Then he did it: he swung himself across the chasm between the buildings, stopped the impact with his feet, and wrapped the rest of the line around his waist to hoist himself into the other apartment. It was embarrassing, the stretch of time he spent splayed on the floor of the room with the cello, recovering his breath.

During these recent concerts, the fear had risen up in him that what he'd taken for a real cello had instead been a recording—how else could one sustain that music without pause? He'd imagined the curtains parting to reveal Pérez, his head looming over the sill to say to Cecilio, "Calm down, that was a record. *Maricón.*" But as he neared the body of the cello that night in his neighbor's apartment, he recognized the instrument as unmistakably real. And he could not, once he'd seen it, imagine the music produced by any other source.

From a bag he carried over his shoulder, Cecilio removed a small pile of rags and a bottle of cleaning solution. He tipped the cleaning solution into cloth and took to the instrument. On the off chance he was questioned that night, or at any point after, he was prepared to say he'd simply been polishing it, that cello which played for him tirelessly, at all hours of the day. But the solution he'd purchased was industrial strength. He'd known, even before his first strokes returned the cloth stained, that it would strip the varnish right off the cello. Until it was utterly naked. Bare as a tomb on Todos los Santos.

This was bliss, his arms in sync with what his untamed brain presented him. In his mind, he watched the letters of Fito's name emerge from the grime with each stroke of the hand:

    O URR
    O URR   CHEZ
FITO URRIBE   CHEZ
FITO URRIBE SANCHEZ

He left when Fito's grave was clean, the cello stripped bare.

As soon as the caravan of fake ambulances had arrived at the base of Mount Saibi, each man in Cecilio's platoon was provided with a fisherman's anchor and rope from the trunk of one of the cars. They began to ascend the mountain, and by afternoon it turned to sheer rock face.

When they finally made it to the front, the energy they encountered was manic, a far cry from the lethargic pace of the bunker. Hundreds of soldiers camped out beneath makeshift shelters. Machine guns stationed at the far end of the mountain-top were manned around the clock.

In the early morning of their fourth day, the shelling began. As a barrage of explosives rained over the front, Cecilio stood and watched them drop. Later, crouched behind a wall of sand-bags, he found Fito busy preparing for the counterattack. He put his hand on Fito's shoulder, and said simply, "*Amigo, así, no puedo más.*"

When Fito refused to join him, Cecilio defected alone, at night.

Also at night, Fito's squad crossed paths with a rogue com-pany of Falange troops forcing their way toward Bilbao. Back in the city, Cecilio learned that the Falange had executed every one of them.

When he told Noemí about the cello, weeks later, he was sit-ting across from her on a train heading into the seaside town of Bermeo. Cautiously, he walked her through each step, including his crude use of the army grappling hook, which he was sure she would dismiss as embellishment. From the train, they watched the changing landscape as they pulled out of Guernica, passed behind the industrial quarter, and began to trace the river. He explained about the grave—how the cello came to feel like the grave—though she hadn't asked for any explanation.

Because Noemí, for her part, loved Cecilio, she listened patiently, though it was crazy, truly crazy, what he was telling her. She had noted that Cecilio had been absent from bed one night, and she had presumed, when she'd heard the moan of the cello the next morning, that Cecilio had somehow been responsible. Halfway through an apathetic concerto the music fell off entirely, and since then, they lived curiously in silence. Still, she couldn't have predicted this: not his clearing the chasm with anchor and rope, nor his damaging the property of another person until it was utterly irreparable. But she loved him, Cecilio, whose haggard face was pressed against the window, from whose sleeve peeked out her mother's beaded bracelet, his chosen substitution for the rosary. And because she loved him, she showed no sign of these reactions.

As they rounded the corner on Bermeo, the river below threw its arms open and released itself to the ocean. They both watched as boundless white-capped waves bucked the wind.

Still, she couldn't make sense of it. Wasn't the cello, if anything, more suggestive of Fito's life? In any case, he'd been executed. Surely he'd been thrown with his comrades into a ditch. The hole, that terrible space between the buildings, was in fact more like Fito's burial site than any tombstone. She assumed Cecilio had made this association too, the ditch and the hole, because of the many times she caught him in the children's room, hovering by the window.

Later, sitting on the stone steps of the sea wall, eating from a jar of olives that they purchased because they'd already gone to a bar and were too poor to go to another, Noemí thought again of the cavity between the buildings. From the moment they'd moved into the apartment, the space had worried her. On one of their first days in the building, while Cecilio had been taking a nap, she'd gone down to the foyer to investigate it. There was a door, she discovered, camouflaged into the wall, and so small she had to bend halfway to fit through. When she stood in the courtyard at the bottom of the hole, the door was again barely visible, covered with the same plaster as the building facade. Still, there was a door. She had needed to know—it wasn't unthinkable that one day there would be a child living in their apartment.

She considered mentioning then how she'd always feared that space, but the wind off the sea was frigid; it flooded her lungs when she tried to speak. They had both abandoned the olives. Cecilio was sitting on the step above her and Noemí placed her head on his lap. On the morning they'd awoken to the whimper of the ruined cello, she'd stood in the hallway as Cecilio listened from the children's room.

"Strange," she had said.

He'd stood up and come over to her, and said, "Strange, yes. But fitting too, isn't it?" He had smiled, and with a bit of grandeur, taken her into his arms. "For this new period that we're in. The beginning of this new period of our lives."

Now, with her head in Cecilio's lap, Noemí lets her brain relax a little bit. There's a way that she can get her mind to rest so that all channels related to Fito are blacked out. From this position, when she peers out at her world, in addition to there being no Fito, there is no longer Cecilio's constant private mourning for him. And for a moment, on the seawall in Bermeo, she allows herself to believe that all of this—the break-in, the paring of the cello until it is nothing, neither a gravestone nor an instrument—has somehow been for her.

RECUERDOS:_____

If you're out in the country and looking to disappear, there's a hole in the field exactly 3 km between _____ and _____ that keeps swallowing up the neighbors' sheep. From the city, too, it's fairly simple to arrive there—not far away a concrete platform sprouts, peerless, from the porous earth. This is your stop—sit by the window, pay attention, and get off the train when it's your turn.

I should add that it's extremely easy, on these days when the sun goes early and, with it, certain features of the landscape recede as though erased completely, to feel yourself already expelled from the world, ejected into _____, this strange, slippery place.

But it was your choice to come here, remember? Your choice to exit the train. Only the platform lamp makes itself vulnerable to you, registers and adapts to your shape. It's very thoughtfully designed, this station—there are no signs, no payphone. And while there certainly are trains that could deliver you back to the city, the landscape only glitches to reveal them at four precise moments throughout the day. And so anyone who's changed their mind about disappearing must now endure it all the same.

RECUERDOS: BERGARA

If you're ever walking in the mountains, and you begin to notice shards of orange plastic scattered through the dirt, wait. Before you picture it—the vehicle swerving off the road, a mirror snapped, the glass collapsing—you should know there are hunters who tread the territory above Bergara. They use those plastic orange discs as their practice prey. Their figures erased by heavy sweaters and dark-colored hunting coats, they're our shadow army, our small brigade, who rise each day to multiply the ghosts.

If this sounds unappealing, I promise, by midday the mountains will have changed their tune. The sun will send those hunters fleeing to their unmarked bars, the sporadic crack of shots replaced by bleats of distant sheep and the long, lazy drone of cows. The buzzsaw, actually, makes a similar sound, and can easily be mistaken for the advance of someone's herd. Though if you're lucky, and the operation occurs on the opposing peak, you'll see them: the trees, one by one, coming down.

And if you wander past a *caserío*, be sure to linger there, outside its window. See what you can smell. It will be obvious, of course, in which house the bread is baked, in which the jam is brewed then distributed at every market in the zone. Keep going—the next home is where I spent two sleepless months, intending to steal no more than a bit of rest, a glass of wine. Instead they brought me to the stable, where we crouched beneath the light of a single candle, and that night and nearly every other, assisted a goat from their herd in giving birth. When, much later, I was invited back for dinner, their kitchen reeked of fresh-cut meat: light, acidic, sour at the turn.

When you tire of it all, the hunters, the cows, and the smells, find the street that goes down the steep side of the slope. Begin your descent. Near the bottom there's a bench that sits at the peak of the curve; after walking that dangerous stretch on foot, you'll be in need of a rest, heaven knows.

Do not stop. *This* is where it happens: the cars losing control, barreling off the road.

ELECTRODOMÉSTICOS

In May 1942, a shipment of peanuts arrived in the port of Bilbao and thrust the starving city into a state of joyless, untamed gluttony. Shells were cracked and discarded with abandon. For several days, all business that took place in the underworld of the city—all trysts, black market sales, clandestine meetings—briefly ceased, as the crackle of those peanut casings beneath one's feet made it impossible to go anywhere unannounced.

It wasn't long, however, before a measure of illicit activity resumed. No more than a week: the amount of time it took the residents to finish off all of the peanuts, and, when they were left with nothing else, to pick the shells off of the ground, and eat those too.

❧

The Arrietas' apartment was full of furnishings unfamiliar to Josu. Two oil paintings adorned the foyer; in the living room, marble-topped tables and imperial wilting plants conspired to send long shadows across the floor. Once inside, one remembered the outside world as imprecise, flat, papered over. Already on that first morning in the Arrietas' kitchen, Josu sensed that if their home did not exist in direct conflict with the rest of the city, then it was, at the very least, an exquisite exception to it.

"*Egun on, maitea,*" Mrs. Arrieta called down the hallway to her husband, who called back to her, "*Zergatik esan didazu sukaldetik 'Egun on'? Zergatik ez zara hona etorri musu bat ematera?*"

"*Eta zure musua nahi ez badut?*" she responded.

Josu had never spoken Basque, and neither, it became clear, had his boss. In the fever of their isolation, the two lonely men devoted themselves to installing the oven. Armed with a random assortment of tools, they strove to articulate their movements as gracefully as Mr. and Mrs. Arrieta produced those foreign sounds. Josu swooped his wrench around a point, attempting to loosen the bolt they had misplaced earlier that morning.

At the far end of the kitchen, Mrs. Arrieta held a length of yellow cloth up to the window above the two men. For a few moments, the room became a shadowless, dimensionless place. Then she dropped the curtain and his boss's face was divvied up again into a multitude of planes. "*Errezelak mozteko zure laguntza behar dut,*" Mrs. Arrieta shouted toward the hallway.

For a moment she received no response, then Mr. Arrieta lumbered into the kitchen and made a violent tug at the yellow cloth, which unfurled over the men and floated to the floor.

Through a veil of yellow, Josu could scarcely make out the bust of his boss: all his features were dulled, as though he were embalmed.

"*Ba al dakite euskaraz?*" Mr. Arrieta asked, when he reeled in the fabric. He stared down at them, then looked at his wife.

"No," she said. "No, it seems like they don't."

"You *do* speak Spanish, don't you?" she said, turning to Josu and his boss. Neither of them answered, and instead remained crouched over the oven like rigid little pawns, saying nothing. Finally Josu managed, "*Que sí,*" and his boss, following suit, started repeating "*que sí, que sí, que sí, sí, sí, sí, sí, sí, sí.*"

Mrs. Arrieta smiled and the clock in the hallway cut in and chimed several times. "Oh, that's wrong," She said, glancing behind her. "One day we'll fix it, maybe tomorrow, but for now, if you have your own watch, that's best."

She turned to Mr. Arrieta, "What shall we make for lunch—a stew? Or maybe we should make soup from those leeks we've been hoarding."

"Leeks?"

Mr. Arrieta wandered over to the icebox, and Josu watched him remove seven leeks one by one. The couple discussed the merits of a leek stew as opposed to simply cooking the leeks on their own over the stove. Mrs. Arrieta turned to the men and said, "We'll need the oven, for that, you know."

Josu's boss told her they would have it ready by lunchtime.

On any regular day, Josu would deliver light bulbs. He had done deliveries in every neighborhood. He'd hauled the bag three-quarters down the length of the Boulevard Urquijo, and he had hauled it up the slopes of Iralabarri, all the way to the very last building before the city became plain, unsettled mountain. At the end of these days delivering bulbs he would return to his boss's small, drooping storefront in the old district—Electrodomésticos Ibañez, if you're ever looking for him—and he would report his inventory back to his boss before he left for the day. Often, as the night collapsed in on him, he would discover he had gotten lost again in the web of the old district's identical alleys, and he would return home to his mother in the dark: sweaty, haggard, and late.

It was boring, delivering light bulbs. It was simple work. When the home was wired correctly, and had suffered no damage, Josu's job was to twirl the bulb into its resting place and let the connection between the plates occur naturally. When the work became more difficult—when the bulb did not illuminate, and he found a wire frayed, or broken—he repaired it with electrical tape. In return for this extra effort he was usually treated to a drink, or on rare occasions to the stone-hard cheese he craved, and had once literally dreamt of.

In the Arrietas' kitchen, a wheel of this same cheese sat dangerously on the edge of the kitchen table. Its round body was split by a long shadow, which fell into the one triangular absence where someone had already removed a slice.

After freeing the misplaced bolts intended to secure the oven's legs to its body, Josu and his boss began setting up the pulley system that raised and lowered an optional cooking hood, a new addition on models built after 1941. The distinction meant little to them, however—neither had ever used a gas oven.

Despite this, they started off that morning with confidence. Once they removed the oven from its crate in the Arrietas' kitchen, they arranged all the excess parts on the kitchen floor: the knob for the gas regulator, the cap mixer, the bell mixer, the grates for the burners, and the sculpted wood handle for the oven door, which, when he ran his fingers down the length of it, felt to Josu like a human bone. Josu cradled it, testing out the truth of this sensation, while his boss began organizing the hardware by size. They'd intended to finish the oven by lunch, though they hadn't counted on the constant presence of the Arrietas, wandering, all morning long, into and out of the room.

Just then, Mr. Arrieta filled the frame of the kitchen doorway with his immense shoulders. "*Non daude bonbillak?*" he asked Mrs. Arrieta, who sat at the kitchen table dicing a small pile of onions into little cubes.

"Those bulbs," she called out, switching to Spanish, "are in the drawer of your desk, where we put them when we returned from the market."

Mr. Arrieta's Spanish was more tentative than his wife's. "The drawer of my desk . . . ," he managed.

"Yes."

"And we never planted them?"

"No," said Mrs. Arrieta. "By the time the season came, we had renounced the balcony. And I read that they don't grow well inside. Besides, the soil we had left was poor, do you remember? It felt chalky in your hands"—and her husband's hands floated up before his face, where they took him by surprise. "And you told me it wasn't worth it anymore."

Mr. Arrieta appeared peeled as a corner of light struck the pocket of his collarbone, and wrapped itself around his neck. He tipped the heavy globe of his head against the doorframe and closed his eyes. Mrs. Arrieta seemed unconcerned. She set herself to the onions again.

When Mr. Arrieta lifted his head, he announced, "The bulbs could still have sprouted. In the desk. They could still have flowered, if we bought them surrounded by soil. Do you remember—"

Mrs. Arrieta stood up suddenly, and on her way out of the room, she collected Mr. Arrieta, the boss, and Josu. When the four of them emerged in a study on the other end of the hallway, Mr. Arrieta extended a trembling hand toward the bottommost drawer of his desk.

The bulbs were bound in burlap, but in several places thin green points poked through the weave. They were passed around so that each of the men held one. When he made himself ignore the scratch of the fabric and prick of the stalks, Josu recognized in the object the shape of his own glass bulbs.

For the rest of the afternoon, the bulbs sat in jars along the kitchen windowsill. At the edges of the cups their rooted bottoms grew warped. All three, when unwrapped, had been punctuated by a crown of stalks, though the growth was in its clumsy, beginning stages. Mrs. Arrieta said it was a shame that after so much time the bulbs appeared like this: still ugly. In response, all three men imagined a garden rising there in the bottom drawer of Mr. Arrieta's desk. In Josu's version, the bulbs erupted in thin, delicate stems, and they curled over the edge of the drawer as though a set of fingers, feeling their way out. Later, as he installed the oven alone, he imagined those stems rising from the bulbs, filling the empty air that hung above the real stalks.

The Arrietas wasted away their time like this, inventing dramas, charades, little skits to punctuate the day. Mr. Arrieta once tried to tickle Mrs. Arrieta, but when she reciprocated, he screamed— in his eyes there was a glint of genuine fear—and he curled up like a dead bug on the floor.

In spite of these distractions, the two men managed to install the pulley system that raised and lowered the stove's adjustable hood. Afterward, Josu and his boss spent a quarter of an hour at the stovetop drawing the chain and watching the hood drop like Phaëthon's chariot falling from the sky. They had rebolted the legs of the oven after the morning's error, and so all that was left for Josu to install—after his boss gauged by the height of the sun that it was late afternoon, and fled up the hill to have lunch with his wife—was the small grid of accessories that they had arranged across the Arrietas' kitchen floor.

Fingers still wrapped around the pulley chain, Josu peered out at the parts. His own mother cooked over a small furnace whose hinged door tended to stick unless one used both hands to yank it open. Inside, unbridled flames curled freely around a metal grate. By no fault of the cook themselves, whatever was placed atop that furnace emerged from the pot coarse and burnt.

On the Arrietas' table, the onions that Mrs. Arrieta had diced sat out beneath a patch of sun, and now the corners of the onion pieces were leathered and tan. Josu wandered over to them, and though they were on the edge of smelling sour, picked up a few pieces and put them in his mouth. That pleasant crunch of something between his teeth—when he closed his eyes, it tasted almost like fruit. He stole a few more pieces from the pile and got to work.

When the afternoon ended without warning, Josu explained to the Arrietas that someone would have to return to finish the installation the next morning. He held in either hand the valves that he spent the afternoon assembling—they would adjust the flow of gas to the oven and the burners, respectively—and he nodded to the T-shaped piece of piping on the floor that would separate their apartment's main gas line into two distinct streams. He stammered through an explanation of the mechanics of the oven, beginning with the route that the gas would take from the yet untouched gas line through the T-pipe into the various chambers of the oven.

During this explanation, Mr. Arrieta's expression betrayed only a vague, far-off dissatisfaction, and after a grunt of acknowledgment, he wandered out of the room. Mrs. Arrieta put her hand to Josu's back and led him away from the half-installed oven, through the hallway to the dim, ornate foyer.

She paused in the doorway then said, "We'd like you, specifically, to come back tomorrow," and squeezed his arm. When she'd turned off the lamp, a streak of moonlight materialized on the kitchen floor and cast angular shadows across the metal boneyard of those remaining parts.

All night, the small amount of onion that he'd eaten at the Arrietas tumbled around in Josu's stomach. The next morning, the aftershocks of nausea sporadically wringing his insides, Josu meandered wearily through the old district and across the river. As he made his way into the elegant streets that began the Arrietas' neighborhood, he developed a tableau of his return to them in his mind:

The two of them would be waiting for him when he reached the door to their building, in a choreographed welcome. "Thank you," Mrs. Arrieta would whisper. And, as he climbed the stairs to meet them and their bodies grew larger and larger before him, he might pick up on something else—the scent of soap, perhaps, or a button not yet done.

"You have returned to us," Mr. Arrieta called. "Josu—"

"Yes, that was his name—" Mrs. Arrieta would say.

"Josu has returned." Mr. Arrieta would extend an arm out to him as he reached the topmost steps, and would hoist him into the daydream that Josu invented for himself.

Instead, she said, "We'd love to have the oven ready by the end of the day."

While he unpacked his tools in the kitchen, Josu sensed Mrs. Arrieta's presence lingering just outside the door. Only once he got to work did she finally step into the room.

"Can I ask you," she paused, "how you feel about your job?"

Josu looked up, considering how to answer this question which he'd never before deemed relevant. "I like it," he said finally. It was true—"It's close to my mother's house. Which means I can go home, sometimes, to take a nap." Mrs. Arrieta hadn't moved from the doorframe. Josu continued, "The work is usually a bit more boring than this, deliveries mostly." Then he added, "You know?" which he immediately regretted for how juvenile it rendered him.

"And your boss?"

"Yes?"

"What do you think about him? He's a good person?" When she began the question, Mrs. Arrieta was looking him directly in the eyes, but at some point her eyes shifted to the arrangement of accessories in the middle of the floor.

"My boss treats me well," Josu answered. "He gave me a job."

Mrs. Arrieta had crouched down and was inspecting the parts up close. "This looks complicated," she said, holding up the cap mixer. Josu nodded. "I assume you haven't had too many people asking for these?" He shook his head.

Mrs. Arrieta stood up. "Well," she said, "I won't distract you," and left the room.

Josu waited until she was completely gone, and then he began connecting the T-shaped piping to the gas line. On one end of the T, he secured the valve that controlled the gas flow to the oven, and on the other end, the one that controlled the flow to the burners on the stove. He worked diligently, and after he secured both, he moved on to attaching the lever that adjusted the height of the shade on the oven's back wall.

In truth, the shade was nothing more than a metal rectangle raised and lowered by a pair of arms. But to the oven's functioning it was critical: when a lever was depressed, the arms would lift, and the shade would rise to let in gas. Once heated, the chamber was sealed off again, and the gas line cut. In that slowly cooling oven one could cook for hours. Josu reached inside to align the top-left corner of the shade with the leftmost arm, and as he fiddled with lining up the two holes, Mr. Arrieta lumbered into the room, dragged a chair from the kitchen table, and sat down beside him.

Nervously, Josu wrung his arm around the wrench and Mr. Arrieta's own arm mimicked him. Together, they crested the arc of a revolution and became caught in a sort of synchronized dance. Later, when Josu stood in order to turn on the overhead light, Mr. Arrieta took his place. With a shaky hand he made a single revolution around the bolt.

"*Norabide ona hartu al dut?*" he asked. The men stared at each other. Then Josu placed his own hand over Mr. Arrieta's to guide him. Soon Mr. Arrieta picked up speed, rotating the wrench with new fervor, and Josu had no choice but to let him continue on his own.

While Josu packed up his bag that afternoon and prepared to leave, Mr. Arrieta ran his fingers over the bolts he'd just installed. The further he leaned, the closer his ear came to touching the oven's slanted front pane, where the gas dials were. Soon the side of his head settled into the space between two knobs. His eyes fell shut.

Josu glanced at Mrs. Arrieta standing in the doorway, who raised her eyebrows and said simply, "He doesn't leave the house." Her expression was illegible, her face swept clean of emotion.

That sadness which lay dormant at the bottom of his stomach shifted its weight and awoke. Once he left the Arrietas' that day, all he'd retain was the memory of their dark, magisterial apartment and that look of Mrs. Arrieta's—that expression that excluded him. He dropped his bag. "One final inspection," he called out, as he crouched behind the oven. Then, working quickly, he detached each of the bolts that Mr. Arrieta had just fastened. He removed the shade for the gas window and slid it into the narrow space between the oven and the wall. Then he stood up, collected his bag, and in a gesture of goodbye, set a hand atop the man's resting skull.

The important thing to remember about that second afternoon Josu spent in the Arrietas' kitchen—as he turned over the oven's last set of bolts in his hand, pocketed them, and left—is that he had intended to install the oven correctly. On the night before they arrived at the Arrietas' door with the crated oven, Josu and his boss had both read through the single copy of the oven manual lovingly, as though it were a book of poems. As though both men took pleasure in poetry.

Josu's boss had been pulling the blinds in the back office of their storefront at the end of the day, bruising the whole place with shadow, while Josu, with his fingertips on the binding, widened the mouth of his shoulder bag. He had almost smuggled the manual entirely inside when his boss spotted him and bellowed to Josu from the depths of his stomach, like an angry foal. His boss charged from the windows, whipping his hands at the bag in sad punches. "Josechu!" he shouted as he snatched the manual. "I hope you take yourself to the ocean and drown deep into hell."

His little, gentle boss.

Josu and his boss shared the manual between the two of them that night. His boss took it home with him first, but promised Josu, when they parted ways outside the storefront, to deliver it to him as soon as he finished. Sometime past midnight, his boss showed up in front of Josu's house and handed it off to him. When Josu's boss left, his papery sleep shirt disappeared into the night like a full moon waning. Josu studied the instructions until morning.

Yes, it would be a mistake to forget all of this—a misunderstanding of all of Josu's intentions—even as Mr. and Mrs. Arrieta loaded their pot full of leathered onions and turnip strips into the oven, and even as the gas shade failed to fall when they depressed the lever. Even as Mrs. Arrieta turned off the gas with the back window open, and their dish of vegetables cooked languidly in the cooling oven, rotting at half the manual's promised speed into a brownish stew, it would be a mistake to forget all of Josu's preparation, and to ignore the hours he spent curled into the narrow swathe of moonlight that cut across his bedroom floor, memorizing the relationships between the oven's skeleton and each of its individual metal parts.

When the call from the Arrietas came in to Electrodomésticos Ibañez the next morning, Josu was reorganizing their dwindling supply of light bulbs in the back storeroom. His boss poked his head in.

"Josechu—" he said. Josu stiffened over the pile of bulbs he was sorting. "The oven is not right."

"The oven is not right," his boss repeated. Then he lowered the receiver for a moment, held out the manual, and said, "I knew I should have come back to finish it with you. Look, I've book-marked the pages . . ."But Josu had already turned from him to gather his things.

The spare key to the Arrietas' apartment was stored in a shallow dent beside their door, three-quarters of the way up the wall. A shard of plaster was placed over it, so that to any passerby it would seem nothing more than a strange assortment of shadows, a series of random cracks. "The doorbell wakes my husband," she said when she showed it to him. "Though I don't anticipate you'll have to come again," she added, casting him an oblique glance. Then she laughed. "Of course, you're welcome to, I suppose, if you'd like." Before Josu could respond, she kissed him on both cheeks and left him there on the landing, staring into the Arrietas' apartment, alone.

In the kitchen, Josu sank before the oven in repentance for his shoddy work the day before. Without looking at what he was doing, his hands went automatically to the arms that were supposed to lift the gas shade—those empty arms that last night had lifted nothing. The solution was fast. He pulled the shade from where he'd hid it behind the oven, and he lined it up with the holes at the end of each arm. He removed the stolen bolts from his pocket. They rolled around on the floor.

As he worked, he slowly became aware of a distant voice leaking from the other end of the hallway. Though Josu would never have claimed to understand Mr. Arrieta, he was nearly correct in imagining the man's heavy skull lolling atop his neck as he struggled to articulate that strange repetition of sounds in the yawning darkness. And he was, in fact, utterly correct in imagining the dirty sunset brushing up against the long white wall of Mr. Arrieta's study. Lowering himself into the plush tomb of the couch, Mr. Arrieta cycled through the words while he stared at that wall and watched, in real time, the slow nightfall that Josu had seen in his mind.

As he wandered home, Josu imagined watching himself from the window above the oven, and—like his boss after he'd delivered the manual—disappearing more with every step.

By the time Josu began his installation of the Arrietas' oven, Electrodomésticos Ibañez had already been advertising ovens in their catalog for several months, though no one inquired about them until Mrs. Arrieta called the shop. Josu's boss was ecstatic when the stacks of the store's new catalog first arrived, nearly double its original length and piled neatly in a cardboard box. He commanded Josu to distribute them. "Everywhere . . . ," he said. "Everywhere!"

Josu wound through the alleys and pressed catalogs beneath the door of every building. Not once, on that delivery, did he experience that recurring sensation of being lost. With the last copy, he climbed the stone staircase that led to the neighborhood above the old district, and from halfway up the steps, he tore pages from the binding and let them coast the breeze to the plaza below.

As he did all this, Josu knew that he was being dramatic. As soon as the last page of the catalog left his hands, he had no choice but to acknowledge this show of joy for what it was: artificial, obviously fabricated.

Josu returned to the shop that afternoon to find that his boss too, had deflated. They spent the rest of the day sitting atop the stack of cardboard boxes in his boss's office, their backs against the graying wall—it was no use trying to sell an oven to a starving city.

When the day came to an end, Josu and his boss slid from the store like twin bodies, or like the same body, splitting.

For the two weeks that Josu cycled through his life without the Arrietas, he lived with their constant presence. Implanted in the act of opening and closing his bedroom curtains was the image of Mrs. Arrieta doing the same: her ghostlike arm rising above Josu's as he straightened the cinched cloth along the curtain rod. When he took a seat, he sensed Mr. Arrieta sitting down beside him. When he spied his mother through the window, as he rose up to their apartment at the end of the day, he felt, though he was sorry to admit it, disappointed not to find Mrs. Arrieta waiting there instead.

Then, late on a Tuesday afternoon, the phone rang, and his boss picked up. The two men met heads over the receiver, where they heard Mrs. Arrieta's voice wilt before them. "Josechu," she said, "come please. Everything was going well, but the oven is out again. The interior part." She paused. The two men remained still. "We've poked around a little, but we just don't know what we're doing."

Neither Josu nor his boss responded until Josu remembered to say, "Yes, Mrs. Arrieta. I'm on my way—" but the line, when he finished speaking, was dead. Josu found his jacket flung over a pile of small appliance bulbs, and left.

The door to the Arrietas' building had been left cracked.

Without hesitation he slid inside and coasted up the single flight of stairs to the Arrietas' front door where he rang the bell several times. Then, remembering what Mrs. Arrieta had said about her husband, he backed up, and scanned the doorway for several moments until he found the triangle of shadows betraying the depth of the wall. He removed the key and, turning the knob, he briefly became Mr. Arrieta, rotating the wrench.

Once inside he went straight to the kitchen. There he found a collection of vegetables strewn across the table. A tomato was sliced in half, leaking its insides onto the yellow cloth that Mrs. Arrieta had held up to the window. Nearby, the three bulbs they had unearthed from the bottom drawer of Mr. Arrieta's desk sat in green, clouded water.

On the phone, Mrs. Arrieta had suggested that the problem was with the interior of the oven, and so Josu first checked the connection between gas line and T-pipe. Then he checked the oven shade, but it looked untouched since he'd reinstalled it. If the Arrietas came back to the apartment and found him in that moment, inspecting their perfect oven, he resolved to tell them the truth, that the only mistakes had come from him. That he had only wished to return to their house in order to find himself in their presence again.

As a final measure, he inspected the gas valve behind the oven. Like everything else, it appeared to be installed correctly. He stood up and went rifling through the kitchen cabinets until he found a box of matches. He pulled one out, lit it, and extended it into the cavity beneath the stove top. Immediately a bright flame erupted then turned blue and steady.

Josu forgot all he had taught himself about the correspondence of one part to another. He forgot all about the order of the bolts he had painstakingly memorized in preparation for that first day. As he pulled his hand from the cavity and blew out the match, he forgot completely about his boss, closing up the storefront alone, and about his mother, sitting by herself in their apartment, about to embark on her evening ritual of anticipating him. Josu sat and watched the flame.

Because there had been nearly no work, and because he'd come with the intention of offering the Arrietas whatever skills he had, Josu turned to the vegetables and filed through all the ways he could possibly use them. The tomatoes were cut. To leave them would mean letting them dry out, depending on how soon the Arrietas came home. He piled them into the pot already on the stove, and then he sat down at the kitchen table and set to chopping up the rest of the vegetables.

Soon, Josu's pot of lentils sat churning over a burner, the tomatoes, onions, and carrots slowly softening in the pot. But then, anyone could make lentils—he felt *paleto*, uncultured and poor, for having jumped to it immediately. And so after the stew boiled through, he searched the kitchen for any ingredients he could continue to cook. In the pantry, he found a head of dried red peppers, which he steamed in a vat of water, beside the lentils. He peeled them and let the dark, wrinkled skin fall to the floor.

The hours unwound themselves. It was almost midnight when Josu finished putting together his crudely composed cake, cobbled together by instinct from flour, salt, sugar, and some eggs he'd discovered at the back of the icebox. Only when he slid the cake into the oven did he feel a sense of atonement, a sense that he'd repaid the Arrietas for what they'd extended to him.

As the peppers cooked over a mild flame, Josu plugged the

sink and filled it up with water. He began to scrub the leftover peelings that clung to the cutting board, and slid into a contented trance.

When the knock sounded, he froze for a moment, hands sunk to the elbows in a mountain of foam. The knock came again. Josu lifted his hands from the sink, dried them on his shirt, and padded quietly down the front hall. He hadn't yet reached the peephole when a man called through the wall, "Open the door."

He said he was looking for Mr. and Mrs. Arrieta.

He said he knew that Mr. Arrieta was a Republican, that he'd led a battalion against the Falange.

He knew that Mrs. Arrieta had erased her husband's name from all registries, that Mr. Arrieta had been hiding there, in that house, since the war.

But by the time the investigator from the city government called the Arrietas a family of goddamn *vascoparlante* bastards, Josu had slipped out of the Arrietas' bedroom window, dropped himself into the alleyway between their building and the next, and begun carving his way home through the dark. He was crossing the arch of the Arenal Bridge by the time the investigator claimed that God lit his cigarettes on the farts of the Basques, and he found the mouth of the staircase that would take him up the hill to his mother just as the investigator made the *m* of *menudo* that began *menudo asco de hombre*. Mr. Arrieta, he said, was a disgusting man.

Josu was in bed by the time the investigator left the Arrietas' building, after two more rounds of pounding on the front door, which woke up the elderly man who lived in the apartment above. He—the elderly man—crippled his body into a ball atop his bed, and cowered under the blanket of the investigator's yells, at the same time as he—Josu—ran his thumb raw over the grooved end of the Arrietas' key, which he discovered in his jacket pocket once he arrived home. And just as the insides of the cake all the way back in the Arrietas' oven finally cohered, a thought half formed in the dimly lit cavern of his skull: it was impolite to hold onto the key to someone else's apartment.

In his sleeping body, Josu's muscles already practiced the act of returning.

RECUERDOS: THE NERVIÓN

What you first must understand is that the land in question is punctured twice: *two* rivers push against their containers, open out into the sea.

The instinct is natural to compare Urdaibai to the Nervión, but many people unfortunately are prone to plain, childish comparisons—size, color, directional flow—and so there remains a chronic misunderstanding of the way these water systems conduct their matters in unison.

What I wish to transmit is that, while Urdaibai is governed by eels, by Eurasian spoonbills, black-tailed godwits, bluethroats and swallows, so too is the Nervión a product of rigorous migratory patterns. Like those spoonbills, which each winter unfurl their cavernous wings and disperse, the women who sell sardines along the banks of the Nervión enact their ritual with piety and a similar clockwork-style precision.

By dawn they will have already churned through the stock

delivered to the port, and assembled enough sardines to last them the afternoon. Their children, sluggish on the solitary march to school, will deliver breakfast. And that horde of tattered blouses, of crudely hemmed skirts, will begin their journey, baskets of fish pinned to their heads. They'll walk, as every day, fourteen kilometers to the center of the city.

Should you happen to live, for example, in Sestao, the descent of the flock upon your town is as clear a sign as any that it's a quarter past eight in the morning. You've indulged too much in sleep. Stick your head out the window and let the women's coarsely performed songs, the salt-heavy air, do their part: rise, buy some sardines.

But then, there are other patterns that may serve you well to organize your day: on the paths that cross the city parks, the creeping stain of runoff from the freshly watered plants can be analyzed to give a fairly precise reading of the hour.

Otherwise, the boats that ferry employees to the steelworks factory begin their circuits at six a.m. If you can, make your way up the mountain: it takes a bit of altitude to appreciate the arc that chain of boats carves against the waves, their relentless dedication to scoring the river's surface.

And if you're ever lost, the factory itself serves as an effective beacon: not even in the heart of the city can you find such density of illumination, such variety in altitude, color, quality of light.

Like the seasonal disappearance of the spoonbills, godwits, the eels, and bluethroats, the departure of those women from the city center communicates certain information about the present moment: what's already transpired and, of course, what's about to come. In the last hours of the afternoon, tucked into corners of local train stations or sprawled across the platform's benches, you can find those women speaking quietly to each other, all addresses now turned inward, inaudible to the public ear. Even their features, after hours of such elasticity, in the waning light are more withdrawn. And so it's easy, at this point, to overlook these women, who will have already begun their slow recoupling with the land. But they're the first and most reliable indicator that one's time is nearly spent.

I've ridden the train with them, from the city center, back out to Santurzi. And amidst their lethargic chatter, their lolling sleepless limbs, I have observed them closely, each more pleasant than my own reflection, and have come to terms—as I rarely do—with the day's end.

SIRENS, 1985

When Aitor Madariaga turned eighteen, he received both his license and a job: he became a driver in the first fleet of ambulances to operate out of the hospital in Galdakao, which had opened, coincidentally, only a couple of hours before his birthday. He cruised into his own party in his parents' apartment with some withered balloons from the reception at the hospital, his employment paperwork, and a certificate from his driving instructor. With his generous lips, and these papers in hand, he kissed both Amaia and her sister on the cheek.

He had known for a long time that he would not go to university, he told them that night, during their first drive together in the ambulance. Nerea sat in the passenger seat, next to him, and Amaia perched in the back, on the low cot she had pushed up against the wall of the cabin. On some later rides she lay down, as though she were the patient, and she listened to the sound of the vehicle's motor, and the ribbon of Aitor and Nerea's conversations as their words bloated and broke up in the breeze.

On that first night, Aitor continued to explain why he wasn't going to school, but Amaia soon lost the trail of his sentence to the open window. All spring they'd been hearing about the cells of insurgents meeting in the deadland between their towns, and by the end of the drive she had convinced herself of the most ludicrous possibility: that Aitor had stayed home in order to join them. It was only later, in their shared bedroom, that Nerea explained to her that Aitor's father managed a hat shop in Bilbao, and that Aitor had been planning to take over the business when he turned eighteen. Instead, his father snubbed him, she said, and passed the whole thing to Aitor's younger brother, Iñaki. Jobless, without any other plans, Aitor became an ambulance driver out of necessity.

"It was mean, and totally distasteful," she said to Amaia that night. "To not even warn him, to one day hire Iñaki to work in the shop, and for Aitor to see them coming home together, both of them in their uniforms."

They were getting ready to go to sleep, and Nerea tossed a nightgown at Amaia, though she knew that her sister, who had been blind for their whole lives, would not react in time to catch it. The nightgown struck Amaia and fell to the floor.

"Sorry," Nerea said. Her voice softened a little. "Anyway, you get it, right? His dad is kind of a bitch." Amaia nodded. Behind her, she heard Nerea get into bed.

"Your chest is getting bigger," Nerea said as Amaia pulled her nightgown over her head. "Did you know that?" And then she said, "And Aitor is cuter than his brother anyway. I know you might not be able to tell, but he is."

For a while, Amaia believed that everyone could not see.

This lasted until age five, maybe six, when one afternoon their parents brought them to the thin, riverside strip of sand in Kanala, at that time frequented only by families and nudists. The former took their children there to avoid the cold, turbulent waters of the open ocean, while the latter preferred the relative anonymity it offered, as it was, by lack of those same qualities, a terrible beach. Sitting out on that sand, Nerea made some comment to Amaia about the sagging breasts of a woman lounging several meters away. Amaia snorted, and whispered, "*Look* at them," in agreement, though at the time she could just barely comprehend that what Nerea had observed with her eyes, Amaia had simply made up the experience of seeing.

Only later, when Nerea shrieked at the sight of a crab thrashing toward them through the sand, and she began yelling, "Get up, Amaia! Don't you see it," did Amaia dazedly awaken to her deficit of sight: she saw no creature coming for her. Nerea was calling out, shrieking from far away, when she sensed the vague form of her mother running back from the shore. She felt her mother collecting her in a pair of long, wet arms. Her dad's voice entered the conversation a while later. He said something like, "*Joder*, what were you doing, leaving her alone." To Amaia, he said, "*Mi gordita cieguita*"— my fat, blind daughter—while he cupped a hand to the back of her head.

In their shared bedroom, when they returned from the beach, Nerea climbed onto Amaia's mattress and crawled over her so that she was sitting on her sister's two stretched-out legs. She put her face up close to Amaia's. "You don't see things," she said. Amaia shrugged. In reality, the incident with the crab added to Amaia's fearful suspicion that Nerea possessed some capability that she did not. But it was annoying to have your sister telling you things she claimed were the rigid, unyielding truth.

Amaia thought of the rest of that afternoon, which she had spent discerning if her knowledge of things in her vicinity came from her vision or from some other clue. She knew what the sand was like because she had held it in her fingers, felt the expansive carpet redistribute itself beneath her as she shifted her bottom around, and felt the separate, individual grains as they seeped into her bathing suit and got caught in the folds of her skin. The water, too, she understood, since she'd bathed in it, and even when it was far from her, she heard it draw itself in and out over the dampened sand. She thought again of the big-breasted woman, whom she had looked for later that afternoon.

She was, again, very young—no older than six—and so it is difficult to say for certain if she did or didn't attribute not finding the woman to the fault of her own eyes. But she did draw her head around, many times, in an innocent extension of hope that the woman might somehow appear to her, a naked Madonna washing up on the shore of her mind.

Back in their bedroom, Nerea told Amaia to close her eyes, and instinctively Amaia did. The flesh lids came down over those wet little balls that she could feel, at times, moving around in her head. "Open them." Nerea's breath was warm. "Did anything change?"

With a new sort of embarrassment, Amaia answered, "No." The room was dark, that she could tell, but *no* was the truth; she could "see" very little, only the dim outline of Nerea's face before her. She let the lids fall back down, and Nerea pressed her two thumbs over them. With the most tenderness she had ever shown toward her sister, Nerea moved around the soft skin that hung over Amaia's eyes.

At Aitor's party, everyone milled about while Amaia sat in the armchair Aitor's parents set up for her in the corner of their living room. From time to time, neighbors would stop by to talk to her, each of them painstakingly articulating their name as though she were at risk of not knowing who they were.

Nerea had abandoned her, unsurprisingly, and over the course of the afternoon Amaia heard her sister's thin, lacelike laughter unspool itself across the room. She could have left with their parents, who stayed for a polite hour and then walked the couple of blocks back to their apartment, but Amaia had spent the morning daydreaming, drifting aimlessly through the narrow channels of her own mind until her mother brought her over to Aitor's party. It was only around other people that she realized she had been lonely. She surprised her parents by demanding to stay.

"Hey." Someone settled onto the arm of her chair. Amaia recognized the voice as Aitor's. When she didn't respond immediately he repeated again: "It's me, Aitor."

"Oh."

"Your sister and I are going to leave. My ambulance—the hospital's ambulance—is outside. They let me drive it home."

"Okay," she said at the same time that he said, "Do you want to come?"

They both laughed a little. "Do you want to come along for a drive," he repeated. Then somewhat sheepishly he said, "A short drive. A quick test, you know."

"A test drive?"

"Yeah, exactly," he said.

"To test the motor of the car that you drove home?" She heard Aitor shift to make way for passing guests. After a series of muttered thank-yous, he brought his head back down to her level.

"Okay, whatever, Amaia. A regular drive. Are you interested in coming along for a regular drive?" Amaia could feel her cheeks flush.

When she said sure, he told her to meet Nerea outside; he would join them in a few minutes. "She's already swiped a bottle of *patxaran* from the booze table," he whispered before he walked away.

As Amaia stepped into the foyer, she registered her sister's presence. "You're coming?" Nerea asked.

"I was invited."

"She was, Nerea, calm down," Aitor called from the top of the stairs, as he closed his apartment door. Out on the street, he led them to his ambulance, where it sat parked against the curb. When they were close enough, Nerea took Amaia's wrist and pressed her palm to the cabin's metal siding. Aitor embarked on a description of each of its features.

"I don't know what horsepower means," Amaia said, as she felt around the two doors at the rear of the ambulance. Aitor was somewhere near the passenger seat, describing the engine to her sister. "Actually," Amaia added, "neither does she."

"That's not shocking to me," said Aitor as he wandered around the side of the ambulance to join her. He unlatched the doors to the cabin. "There's not too much back there right now. A bed, basic hospital things, you know, thermometers. . . . We hung a stretcher up on the left-hand wall the other day, and then there's some needles and some blood pressure stuff over there."

Nerea's laugh came from just behind Amaia. "You know nothing about medicine."

"And you," he replied, "know nothing about cars."

"Please, let's just drive," said Amaia. She was unaware that during this exchange, Aitor's fingertips lingered over her sister's waist.

Nerea detached herself from Aitor and led Amaia around to the passenger seat, but when the two of them attempted to fit inside, half of Nerea's body hung out of the ambulance.

"No way," said Aitor. "No way you two are doubling up," he repeated, when Nerea began to climb onto Amaia's lap. "I can't see for shit out of my right mirror, besides, one pothole and someone's head goes flying through the roof," he pointed upward, "and this turns into a real emergency." For a moment neither of them moved, and then Amaia slid past her sister and jumped down to the pavement.

"Don't *do* things like that, Amaia," Nerea called after her. "You're going to hurt yourself!"

But Amaia was already fumbling with the latch to the back cabin. Aitor came around to open it up for her, and she found her way onto the cot pushed up against the wall. She stretched out. It was true, she'd been relegated to the patients' quarters, but as she moved her hands over the starched hospital sheets, she grew distracted by the miracle that this was not the same bed where she'd spent her lonely morning lounging. As the engine started, and the ambulance shuddered over a slew of potholes, she felt thankful, oddly, that she couldn't see. She was freed from having to watch them leave town on the battered roads that fled Lemoa.

In fact, she didn't have to imagine them tethered to any road, anywhere.

As they approached a steady speed and the afternoon sloughed its way to night, and as the last hints of sun played themselves haphazardly off the dim glass windows of the city's apartment buildings, Amaia wound her fingers tight around the cot's metal frame. She was the only one of them, that afternoon, capable of experiencing the ambulance casting off into a vast, formless nothing.

Aitor worked at the hospital until ten p.m., three days a week. Most nights after his shift he would drive to their apartment and idle until they emerged. It began as a jest: when Aitor dropped the sisters off after that first night, he joked that they would need to see each other again in order to finish their stolen bottle of *patxaran*, but after their second or third drive together the bottle was done, and by then it was clear he needed no excuse to come back: Nerea and Aitor were together.

They would flirt in the front part of the cabin, and when Aitor dropped them home at night, Amaia would climb down from the back of the ambulance, and outside their building, she would hear Nerea's distant laugh pooling behind the rolled-up window. Sometimes they kept her waiting long enough that she took a seat at the bottom of the stairs leading up to their apartment. Once, Nerea, a little drunk, asked Amaia why she had stared at them while they kissed that night.

After that, at the very least, they all knew where they stood with each other. Nerea and Aitor kissed freely in the front seat— Amaia could hear them—and she called them *burros besándose* whenever she lost control of her own jealousy. Kissing donkeys. Aitor found it hilarious, and so Nerea did too.

The ambulance belonged to the hospital, but its first weeks of operation were so disorganized that no one, as far as Aitor could tell, kept track of who drove which vehicle when. After they let him drive the ambulance home from the opening reception he planned to return it to the hospital, but when he punched out after his first real night on the job, he couldn't find anyone who could tell him where to leave it. There were only two other ambulances parked at random, each on opposite sides of the lot. He wandered the hospital for another hour in search of his supervisor, but half the building was still unfurnished, and in those empty rooms he found no one. Eventually a janitor told him to stop being a bigheaded hero, and to drive the ambulance home. Each time he returned to the hospital, he became less and less inclined to leave it there, until the vehicle in effect became his, and he became associated with it, and the people who knew him in Lemoa would have been more shocked to one day find him behind the wheel of his father's old sedan.

"Either way, it doesn't really matter. I'm the best driver. They love me," he said to Amaia and Nerea. "If I ever met my supervisor while I was out driving, before even mentioning the ambulance, he would say to me, '¡Coño! ¡Aitor! Give my regards to your mother, what's up, what's new with you, man, could you use a smoke?'"

It was late May, one of their early drives, and the three of them were deep in the countryside: Nerea had ordered Aitor to take them far away from town so she could see the ambulance's flashing red lights in action. Amaia dragged herself out of the back of the cabin and came around to the side of the road to join her. She slid her head into the space beneath her Nerea's jaw, and Nerea, keeping her eyes on the roof of the ambulance, set her chin atop Amaia's ear. In the front cabin, Aitor fiddled with a set of controls.

When the siren erupted down the empty street, Amaia seized Nerea, and they both screamed. They didn't even hear Aitor switch it off because they were busy wailing in high-pitched unison to the exact rhythm of the alarm.

"If I run into my supervisor tonight," Aitor said to them when they had gotten themselves back into the ambulance, "I can at least tell him that I *am* on duty, following up on a call about two psychotic sisters."

They'd been together—Nerea and Aitor, and Amaia in the back too—for almost two months when Aitor asked if they wanted to spend a weekend at his uncle's summer flat in Ea. "Don't be stupid, you're my sister. Of course you'll come," Nerea had responded when Amaia clarified that she was invited too. They were alone in the kitchen, cleaning up after lunch while their parents retired in front of the TV. Amaia was about to begin washing the stack of dishes piled in the sink when Nerea came over, took her wrist, and gently held a plate between her sister's fingers until Amaia closed her hand around it. Then Nerea added, "We like having you."

Amaia felt a hard germ of frustration budding in her. If she hadn't so feared being left at home, she might have said something dangerously mean, or else dropped a plate. Instead, she nodded once, rinsed it, and allowed Nerea to hand her a new one. She restrained herself from reminding Nerea that she could do the dishes without any help.

A few nights before they left for Ea, they were out in the ambulance, when Nerea made Aitor pull over to the side of the road so she could run into the forest and pee. The door of the cab slammed closed, and Nerea's footsteps padded the ground as she disappeared into the trees. After a few moments, the sounds of Aitor's shallow breathing separated out from the white noise of the ambulance. Amaia estimated she had only a few minutes—if that—before her sister came back. And then with an ease that surprised her, she asked Aitor if he thought she was attractive.

"Excuse me?"

His clothing rustled as he shifted his weight in the front cab.

Amaia hesitated, then repeated herself: "Do you think that I'm pretty? Objectively, I mean."

Aitor laughed nervously.

She said, "It's just—how am I supposed to know what I look like, you know?" Amaia felt the blood rise in her face as she pushed her way through the lie. The thought of Nerea returning from the woods to discover this exchange made her feel faint. Despite that, she continued, "I just wonder if you'd be willing to describe what you see when you look at me?"

Aitor seemed to have gone completely still. Even his breathing was no longer traceable. For a few minutes, she could discern no evidence of him in the ambulance at all. It had been a mistake, of course, to let her desire become legible—that was now clear. And so she began a process long familiar to her: she blocked out all sensory input piece by piece so that soon enough she'd be sealed off in a vacuum of her own making. She had almost completely detached herself from reality when Aitor said, "Well, you have kind of normal, brown hair."

Amaia smiled. Tentatively, she asked, "Do you think it's pretty?"

"Yes," he said after a moment. "I think it's pretty."

"Go on." As he continued to describe her face, feature by

feature, Amaia bloomed with a simple, guiltless pleasure. She felt no remorse for asking him to perform this exercise that she and Nerea came up with as children. And, contentedly, she feigned appreciation for the descriptions he provided, even though Nerea had served as her mirror for years—ever since they'd both understood she was blind. Because of her sister, Amaia had understood what she looked like her entire life.

Aitor stopped abruptly in the middle of describing her mouth. A moment later, Nerea climbed into the cab and Amaia sensed his attention shift back to her sister, but it didn't matter: she had felt his eyes on her, as evident as physical touch.

Several days later, he parked his ambulance around the corner from their apartment, and after parting with their mother, the two sisters piled their weekend bags into the back cabin, and shoved them beneath Amaia's cot.

In the living room of Aitor's uncle's flat, on the Friday night they arrived, Aitor took a full bottle of *patxaran* out of his bag. It was Aitor's first time drinking around them—he only took measured, occasional sips when responsible for driving them all home—and that night, once he surrendered to the influence of the liquor, a dormant goofiness erupted. His laughter was manic, clownish. It was clumsy and unattractive. He couldn't manage to get his sentences out without them imploding. Like a cartoon character he began, "Don't you think it's in*sane* that my dad said he'd hire me and then—"

He lost it again. He sputtered and made a sound like a fake cry, and then his laughter got muffled, and Amaia sensed he had pressed his mouth against some fabric, or some other person. Several minutes passed before he collected himself and emerged from Nerea's shoulder.

Instead of asking his uncle's permission to use the apartment, Aitor had brought them there in secret, before his uncle arrived. That was how they had ended up at the beach on the last weekend in May. In the week leading up to their trip, bursts of rain had ruptured every day. Out on the sand, the sun did little to cut the chill of the wind as it coasted over their exposed stomachs.

The three of them had all been sleeping next to each other on the pull-out mattress in the apartment, and though Amaia was fairly sure that she heard Nerea adjusting herself in Aitor's arms at night, they never tried anything more around her. On the second afternoon at the beach, Amaia was lying on her back, caught up somewhere in her own mind. She was paying no attention at all to Nerea and Aitor, until Nerea came over to her and put her mouth to Amaia's ear.

"Aitor and I just had sex," she whispered. Down at the shore, distant waves slapped the sand. "You probably didn't even realize, did you?"

She was right. Amaia had no idea where Aitor even was.

Later that afternoon, on the drive home, Amaia lay down on the cot, pulled back the starched top sheet, and burrowed into it, though she had promised Aitor, when they first rode in the ambulance, that she would not.

One Sunday afternoon in early June, Aitor tried to teach Nerea how to drive. Amaia drummed a pattern onto the side of the cabin as he explained the different positions of the gears. Nerea was getting them mostly correct. She faltered on shifting between the third and fourth, but soon she got comfortable enough for

Aitor to suggest that she try driving solo.

"I'm going to be a patient who's called you, okay," he said to Nerea. "You're going to pick me up."

Nerea giggled. "I think you've already picked *me* up, haven't you?"

Both Amaia and Aitor rolled their eyes—several years ago, Nerea taught Amaia to do this, calling it a critical social skill—but Aitor had his eyes on Nerea and not on the rearview mirror, and so the moment passed without either of them realizing they mimicked each other. Amaia heard the door slam, and then Aitor's voice came from somewhere outside of the ambulance. She climbed out of the back and took his spot in the passenger seat.

"Okay," Amaia heard him begin, and then his voice grew increasingly muffled.

Amaia squeezed her sister's shoulder in a show of solidarity. "Get ready," Nerea said, but for a while—Amaia couldn't tell how long—they sat there, totally still. Then all at once the whole ambulance jolted forward and for a few uninterrupted seconds they were accelerating violently, faster than Aitor had ever driven them. When Nerea slammed the ambulance to a stop, Aitor's yells floated to them from down the street.

"Nerea! Goddamn it!" he screamed. His voice was shattered, cut through with heavy breathing. When he caught up with the ambulance, he yanked the passenger door open and flung his heaving chest across their laps. Amaia shrieked at the unexpected weight.

"Sorry, Amaia," he said, as he pulled himself across both their sets of legs. Then he flipped over onto his back, so his head rested on Nerea's thighs.

"My god, he's crossing his arms over his chest like he's a corpse!" Nerea said. "Get up, Aitor," she yelled, and Amaia felt his body flop around atop them as Nerea jabbed at his shoulders. "Get up," she repeated. "You're being so weird!" Amaia felt his chest lift, and he took her hand.

"I'm back from my deceased state," he wheezed, "to remind us all that Amaia would be a much better driver than her older sister." Nerea quaked with giggles, but Amaia took Aitor's hand to her mouth and kissed it gently. She said very solemnly and without a smile, "Blessed father, here lies Aitor Madariaga." She paused. The peak of Nerea's cackle erupted. "May he rest in eternal peace."

Soon summer came to Lemoa—real summer—and with it the series of festivals that seemed to crop up every weekend in a different town. While the celebrations began tamely enough, by nighttime the sky was scarred with fireworks, the ground with beer, wine, Coke, and trodden streamers. No one seemed to remember which saint they were supposed to be celebrating on any particular night, if they remembered the festivals were dedicated to saints at all. Amaia's parents loved to retell the story of the drunken man they'd heard proclaim, "Who was that whore Magdalena, anyway?"

That next year, someone fell from a cliff into the sea.

Amaia, knowing all this, had been content to stay at home. Nerea would often stay with her, but that summer, as soon as the season started, sometime in June, she and Aitor took to chasing the parties, leaving the house at ten p.m., driving from town to town, and not arriving home until five or six the next morning. Sometimes Nerea sidled into bed beside her sister when she returned. Often she woke Amaia, or intended to wake her, not knowing that most nights Amaia lay there sleepless until she heard the ambulance's motor pause beneath her window.

One night, Nerea slid into bed next to her and put her mouth to Amaia's ear.

"Amaia."

"Yes."

"Amaia," she said. Her breath reeked of wine.

"I'm awake. What?"

Nerea gripped her sister's arm. "Look at me." Amaia turned over to face her and Nerea took a deep breath. "I lied to you. On the beach, at Aitor's apartment."

"Oh?"

"We didn't have sex then." Nerea paused. "I just . . . made it up." She kissed her sister's shoulder through the cloth of her nightgown. A relief invaded Amaia; the force of it embarrassed her slightly. As the two of them lay there beside each other, she became aware of all the points of contact between them and Amaia hoped that her sister had not noticed her body relax at the news. After a few minutes, however, Nerea lifted her head and said, "Actually, we just did."

When Amaia asked where, Nerea had already turned over. Facing away from her, Nerea answered lazily, "In the ambulance, on the cot."

In the middle of one of those nights in heat of the summer, when Amaia was perpetually being left at home, she woke up and felt the surface of Nerea's bed to find her sister was still out. It was silly to have expected her there, when at that hour she'd certainly be next to Aitor in the ambulance, the two of them winding along some mountain road in between parties. For a moment her mind swerved out of control and she could not escape the image of another driver turning the bend to discover the ambulance accordioned, wreathed in smoke.

With the vision of the crash having ruined her chances of sleep, she stood up and decided instead to get some air. Going for a walk at night—something she had never done before—was, for her, its own kind of rebellion. And rather than the faint jealousy she'd felt toward her sister all summer, she felt instead a solidarity.

She had just reached the foyer when she heard Nerea whisper, "*Amaia.*" It was one of those theatrical whispers that sounded out of place in real life. "What are you doing?"

"I was just going for a walk."

"Do you know what time it is?"

"No," said Amaia. "You know that I can't tell on my own."

"But you know that it's very late, right? We just got home."

"It's dark out. I'm not dumb, Nerea."

From outside, Aitor's voice called to them: "Amaia, is that you?"

"Yes, it's me," she yelled back. The sense of solidarity had vanished. This time she couldn't withhold the resentment from her voice. Aitor, in response, laughed his restrained, self-aware laugh.

"We've missed you." Amaia turned toward Nerea, who said, "Yeah."

"Come back," Aitor called. "I'll pick you both up. How about tomorrow? Would that be okay?"

"Sure," Amaia said. "That would be okay." Nerea grabbed hold of Amaia's arm as though to drag her up to the apartment, and in defiance, Amaia called out louder, "OKAY, Aitor." She was poised to yell "I'VE MISSED YOU TOO" but Nerea, slightly drunk, had begun to giggle. They left Aitor at the curb with no goodbye, and climbed the stairs, each attempting to quiet the other's laughter and her own.

In the spirit of their first expedition, they pilfered a bottle of liquor from their parents' kitchens and took it out only when they parked far away from town on one of the unlit country roads.

Amaia continued to ride on the cot, but she spent her first ride back in the cabin convincing herself that Aitor had changed the sheets since the night he and Nerea spent there several weeks before. On one of their early rides he had told her that he hadn't taken a single person to the hospital since it opened. "This whole ambulance is in pristine condition," he'd bragged. "Never been touched."

At least one point of obvious progress had been made since Amaia last joined them: Aitor discovered how to turn on the red emergency lights without setting off the siren too. Now, as soon as they made it far enough outside of town, Aitor parked and then they all soundlessly withdrew from the ambulance and reassembled beneath its muted glow. Somehow the feeling had welled up amongst the three of them that they were an insepara-ble trio, mistakenly parted.

Several nights into this new tradition, Nerea, Aitor, and Amaia sat outside the illuminated ambulance, playing their own erratic version of the game Would You Rather. At times they adhered to the rules and began their questions with "Would you rather," but more often they deviated from the original game entirely.

"If you could have any feature of a cat, what would it be?"

Amaia meant it as a serious question, but it came out like a joke.

"You're kidding," Nerea said.

"Not at all."

"Physical features?" Aitor asked.

"What else do you think 'features' refers to?" said Nerea.

"I don't know, spiritual features?" Amaia said. "I don't care, you decide."

"Hm, okay." Aitor clicked his tongue while he thought. He said finally, "I would want to live as though I had nine lives."

Nerea said, "So you want nine lives."

"No, I want to feel as though I have nine lives. It's different."

"It's a *spiritual* feature of a cat," Amaia said.

"Exactly."

"I don't see why you wouldn't just wish for nine lives—"

"We're not wishing," said Amaia. "It's not a wishing game."

"She's right," Aitor said. "It's about making a mental change—"

"A spiritual change," Amaia added.

"Spiritual!" he repeated, his pronunciation beginning to slur. "It's about changing what's in your head, and . . ." They waited as he groped for the end of his sentence. "In your *soul*." Amaia had lost track of where the bottle was until she heard Aitor swallow emphatically after he spoke.

"I'm sorry. I still don't see the difference," Nerea said. Aitor passed the bottle to Amaia.

"Okay," he began. He was obviously drunk. "It's about . . ."

"Being reckless?"

"No. Well, I don't know . . . it's hard to explain—"

"No, it's not." Amaia cut in. "It's just about fear. About not being afraid of things. Try not to be so dense, Nerea."

She waited for a response. After a long pause, Nerea said, "Okay."

"What?"

"It's your turn." Nerea sounded subdued. "Which 'feature of a cat' would you adopt?"

Amaia wondered if she should say what she was thinking. She felt warm and, with the effects of whatever stolen cooking liquor they had been drinking, almost weightless. And for the first time she felt completely comfortable in the presence of Aitor and her sister.

"Fine," she said. "Their eyes."

For a long time, they sat together in the dark. Amaia could hear Aitor picking at the label on the bottle, and behind them, the trees shifting their weight. In the distance, the hum of a car engine grazed the night. Nerea, whose own frustration had been softened by her sister's answer, drew her palms back and forth across Amaia's shoulders.

And then all of a sudden came the screech of acceleration, the thwack of contact, and a cacophony of shattering glass. They all started. Nerea grabbed her arm, and from her other side, Aitor mumbled, "What the hell . . ."

"That wasn't . . . ?" Amaia began.

"No," Nerea said. "No, it wasn't the ambulance."

Softly at first, a strange, pleading moan emanated from the place of the accident. The three of them sat there, listening, as though they would only know what to do once the noise had finished. But it continued, and over time distinct strains joined and left the accumulation, until what had at first sounded like one person seemed instead to be many. Amaia sensed both Aitor and her sister tense up beside her. After a moment, she heard them too: the uneven shuffle of footsteps, lurching down the road.

"My friend, can you tell me," the man called out, "if that's really an ambulance that you have there."

Aitor snapped to attention like the dutiful hospital worker he'd been trained to be. "*Joder*," he said. "Yes, it's an ambulance. Oh god, get in, get in." Amaia listened to him guide the man around to the ambulance's back doors. Once the man was strapped into the cot, he thanked Aitor. And then he paused, and this time his speech came out thinner, markedly depleted: "Would you mind going to get the rest of us?"

"Right," Aitor jumped out of the ambulance and slammed the back doors. As he sprinted around to the driver's seat, he shrugged and called out to Nerea, "Follow me?" Then he sped down the street, passed through a roundabout and turned a corner.

When she and Amaia came upon the site of the accident a few minutes later, Nerea yelped. Beside the ambulance lay a mangled car. Flipped over, a kilometer or two down the road, was a second. One of the men tangled in the wreckage repeated a series of hoarse incantations: *Jesus, God, and Mary, Mother Mary, Kind Virgin Mary, Mary Our Mother, Mary, Mary, My Virgin Hope . . .*

But even worse was the back cab of the ambulance, where six of the eight injured men already lay, some unconscious, their bodies folded up and contorted in order to leave room for the rest. While Nerea joined Aitor in extricating the last two men, Amaia listened to the chorus of their labored breathing. One of them called out to her, "Don't be shy, there's room for one more." Eventually, she heard Aitor shut the doors and struggle to secure the back latch. He rushed past her on his way to the driver's seat.

"Wait," Nerea yelled after him. "Where will Amaia sit?"

"I don't know," Aitor said. He had the door open, and was poised to hoist himself in. "The back is full. You saw that." He got quiet. "Did you hear them? I don't want to put your sister in there."

"Well, she can't walk home," Nerea said. "You know she can't see."

"I'll walk home," Amaia called out. "I want to walk." She had been trailing their voices, and she kept a hand on the cabin as she edged toward them. Aitor watched her for a moment, then he said, "Jesus Christ." He grabbed Amaia's wrist and dragged her around to the front door, where he placed her foot on the cabin floor and raised her into the seat by her waist.

Nerea called out Aitor's name while Amaia settled into the ambulance, and Aitor hurried back to the driver's side. He flipped on the siren, all at once frighteningly calm, and that familiar throbbing sound tumbled around them as he said to Nerea, "You can see that there's no room for you. Amaia can't walk home, okay?"

It was better that Amaia could not see her sister's face when Aitor said, "You will."

Nerea was still calling his name when they pulled out onto the road, made a careful three-point turn, and fled.

On the drive to the hospital, Aitor began to whimper, though he sounded not like the men lying restless in the back cabin, but instead like a mewing calf, or like his neighbor's wounded dog, whose chewed-up testicles, after he lost a fight with some other Lemoan hounds, had become the shame of the whole block.

Every so often, Aitor repeated, "My god, oh my god."

There, from the front seat, housed in the intimate brain of the ambulance, Aitor's voice sounded exponentially nearer than it had from the back. Amaia could hear each of the involuntary noises that escaped him, and he seemed unbearably close. As they drove, the sense of gravity peeled away from her, and she felt, filtering through her limbs, an extension of that same dizziness she had experienced when Nerea first tried to teach her how to roll her eyes. Her sister's instructions were poor and imprecise, and so instead of tracing an arc with her eyes, Amaia had accidentally rolled them back into her head. Caught between the inside of herself and the outer world, she had felt her whole skull radiate with a painful, feverish warmth. Beside Aitor, the feeling revived itself in every part of her body.

When the ambulance finally slowed to a stop, Aitor told Amaia they had made it to the hospital, and that he would be back. She listened to him unlatch the doors to the cabin, and to the men's moans gradually floating out of the ambulance and away. While she waited for him, she was reminded of the nights when Aitor and Nerea first got together that ended with her waiting alone on the steps to their apartment. She had sat there while they messed around in the two front seats, and when she realized they were the same front seats where she now sat, the desire bloomed again behind her eyes.

After an infinite stretch of time, the door opened and Aitor slid into the driver's seat.

"How are they?"

"Not great," he said.

"Do you think they'll all be fine, though?"

He hesitated. "I think whoever comes out of that hospital is

not going to have a lot in common with the person who went in."
The ambulance was silent as Aitor sat looking up at the half-lit
building. He started the motor. "Fine, maybe. But different."

"Do you think the crash was an accident?" Amaia asked him.

"What do you mean?"

"It just sounded suspicious to me, I don't know. That car
going full speed . . . ," she said. "But maybe they were just drunk."
She felt Aitor turn out of the hospital parking lot. "Anyway, it
could have been a lot worse, couldn't it? Nobody died."

"Yeah, I guess not," he said absentmindedly, but then his
voice hardened and he said, "Jesus, Amaia. I think they came
close enough."

Later, when Aitor pulled up beside Nerea on the outer edges
of their town, maintaining, pathetically, that he hadn't truly
abandoned her, she had said nearly the exact same thing: "Maybe
you didn't—but don't you think you came close enough?"

As they pulled out of the hospital parking lot and merged
seamlessly onto the deserted road that ran between Galdakao
and Lemoa, Amaia was quiet. Aitor's comment had injured her
briefly, but it hadn't been enough to dim the memory of the last
time they had been together in the empty ambulance, when he
had traced every feature of her face. With the men finally gone
from the back cabin, she reveled in each of these new moments
alone. Amaia only realized they'd been speeding when the right
half of the ambulance dropped off the side of the road. As it
clamored back onto even ground, the whole cabin rattled. Aitor
slapped the dashboard and said, "*Mierda*. Impossible to see anything through this goddamn fog."

Yes, Amaia thought, succumbing to a small swell of sympathy

for him, it's impossible to see anything. And then, sitting there beside Aitor as he tore toward their town, and toward Nerea, Amaia halfheartedly ran over the attempts at conversation she rehearsed while she sat in the parking lot, waiting for him. The jumbled collection of words she planned to say at the end of the drive that she hoped might somehow make Aitor consider, instead of her sister, kissing *her*.

After a while the ambulance made a series of short turns, indicating they had reached Lemoa. Though Aitor could have allowed Amaia to stay there beside him as he searched for her sister, he drove her straight to her parents' apartment instead. When they arrived, he told her she was home. He was cold, purposefully, and Amaia felt, for the first time, like one of his patients. Still, she had lingered briefly before getting out, hoping that Aitor might say something else. But he was silent, and in the end there was nothing special about the few short moments that they shared in the ambulance, in front of her house.

AUTHOR'S NOTES

Personal Connection

Hanging up on the walls of my childhood home were dozens of the paintings my grandfather made of his native Euskadi, known also by its names in Spanish (País Vasco) and English (the Basque Country). One of those paintings is the cover of this book. All of them, however, are the source of intertwining fascinations for me: my grandfather's life, the region itself, and an aesthetic practice that bypasses realism to find truth in the folkloric.

My maternal grandfather was from Bilbao, the industrial heart of the Spanish Basque Country, where he had a joyful childhood before the outbreak of the Spanish Civil War. A member of the Republican forces, he fled the country on a fishing boat following Franco's victory, and eventually arrived in New York, where he met my grandmother, a first-generation American Jew who'd grown up in Brooklyn. Together, they returned to the Basque Country many times, though they never lived there comfortably during Franco's dictatorship, in part because of my grandfather's Republican past. Still, my grandmother adored these trips and the time spent with my grandfather's loving and expansive family. And so she became the keeper of their stories, listening with intent to their experiences during the war and the period afterward. Coupled with my grandfather's paintings, my grandmother's meticulous recordkeeping kept the memory of his ancestry, and his home territory, alive. They also endowed the region with a mythical quality.

Growing up in suburban Boston, I was fascinated by this personal connection to a place so far removed from what I knew. My first trip to the Basque Country, when I was six years old, confused me—it seemed impossible that we could have family who were so utterly different from us—but a return at age eighteen began a decade of frequent visits, deepening relationships with my mother's many cousins, and collecting the anecdotes and observations that would become a part of these stories.

While writing the book, I've felt both inside and outside of its subject matter. I've been privy to private stories and experiences as a result of my parentage, while remaining culturally American. As a writer, to be slightly outside of a place can be wonderfully perspective-breaking: every normal detail is made new before your eyes. Still, to be an outsider is a great responsibility, and my intention is to write with nothing but deep respect and admiration for the Basque Country, a place that my family may be *from*, but I am not wholly *of*.

It may also be worth acknowledging that my very Irish name comes from my father, who grew up in Northern Ireland during the Troubles, a period which saw terrible bloodshed at the hands of several terrorist groups. Writing about the Basque Country, particularly during the years of ETA (Euskadi Ta Askatasuna), has also been a roundabout way of engaging with the history of the Troubles, a topic that felt perhaps too near and too painful to write about head on.

Many of my grandfather's paintings feature angels that are a composite of person and bird: a human head attached to an avian body. It may be obvious (spelled out in the epigraph!) that Italo Calvino is a huge influence of mine, but the original fabulist for me will always be my grandfather. As such, I found it impossible to write about the Basque Country without indulging in this style. And so, given that these stories are neither nonfiction, nor are they, at all times, *realistic* fiction, I think it bears addressing some of the decisions made in their construction.

Historical Treatment

The stories in this collection are all set during the fifty years following the Spanish Civil War. The two earliest stories, "Electrodomésticos" and "No Spanish," take place during the 1940s, whereas "Flock" and "Northern Spain, 1985" take place in the 1980s. In most cases, the fabulist elements of the text do not affect the underlying history. Below, I've outlined the few exceptions to this rule:

"No Spanish"

The first and most important thing to point out about this story is that it is an inversion of what happened to so many: they were forced to exchange Basque for Spanish as a result of the cruel prohibition of regional languages. Although the narrator misses Spanish, rather than Basque, this is of course by no means a reflection of my own stance with regards to language. Rather, situating the story this way allowed me to write what I felt were more interesting tensions around nationalism into the characters' family lives. It's my hope that everyone familiar with this period of history—and perhaps even those who aren't—will see this inversion lurking immediately behind the text.

The radio station in this story is based on the famed Radio Euskadi, the key clandestine Basque radio station that broadcast first from Iparralde, in the French Basque Country, then later from the Venezuelan jungle. Whereas the narrator in this story complains of hearing no Spanish on the clandestine radio station that her father listens to, during this period Radio Euskadi indeed had programming in Spanish and Basque.

"Recuerdos: Lemoa"

Two buildings are featured in this story: a cement factory, which very much exists in Lemoa (Cementos Lemona), and a convent housed in an old paper mill, which does not. The convent was based, however, on several convents housed in contemporary buildings that I observed around Bilbao. The buildings to me looked mundane and not particularly holy—one reminded me of an American office park—and I became interested in what I found to be a strange aesthetic contrast between the purpose of the buildings and their facades. The paper mill in the story is inspired by the paper mill in Durango, just ten miles away from Lemoa.

"86 Ways of Becoming Juan Manuel Berastegui"

Like the cloister in Lemoa, Juan Manuel Berastegui is also a composite. Certain influence was taken from the writer Txillardegi, one of the original founders of ETA, who fled to France. Txillardegi left the Basque Country in 1961. And while the fictional Juan Manuel remains in the Spanish Basque Country until 1966, participating in the group's early attacks, he resigns from ETA in 1967, just as Txillardegi did, out of disagreement with the group's commitment to armed struggle. In *The Basques: The Franco Years and Beyond*, historian Robert P. Clark also profiles an unnamed early member of the group whose story and trajectory (apart from a literary career) are similar to that of Txillardegi.

Gonzalo, on the other hand, believes that he's been hired to join some version of the UAR (Unidad Acción Rural), a subunit of the Civil Guard founded in 1978 and dedicated to tactical counterterrorism efforts. The UAR, however, didn't yet exist in 1976, when Gonzalo's story is set, and he is hired as a regular civil guardsman. His decision to police the speaking of Basque is particularly silly because by 1976 the prohibition of banned languages would have, in practice, long expired: a year prior, a decree was issued allowing Euskera to be taught after hours in state primary schools.

A Note on Sources

A number of historical sources supplemented my family history and experiences in the Basque Country. While these sources were wide-ranging in nature, and to a degree in political stance, I leaned heavily on the work of historians Robert P. Clark and Paul Preston, for excellent neutral accounts of the rise of ETA and the Spanish Civil War, respectively. Also indispensable were two Spanish-language texts: Pio Baroja's *El País Vasco*, originally published in 1953, and *Una Breve Historia de Euskadi* by José Luis de la Granja, Santiago de Pablo, and Coro Rubio Pobes, published in 2020.

About the Basque in this collection

The Basque sentences that appear in this collection were translated by Aritz Branton from English to Euskera Batua, or

Standard Basque. While numerous regional dialects exist in the Basque Country, Standard Basque, developed in the 1960s, is the language of official communications: the language in which news is reported, students are educated, and books are published. In accordance with this, the Basque sentences in these stories appear in Standard Basque, despite some variation in characters' historical and geographical context.

Acknowledgments

I owe thanks to so many for helping me bring this book into the world. First off, to Kristen Renee Miller, for her belief in it, and then to Bret Johnston, who coached me through writing the earliest version of it eight years ago, when it was still my undergraduate thesis. That fall and winter is to date my most productive writing period and I couldn't have produced any of it without his enthusiasm and guidance.

I'm also grateful for the funding that I received for that early iteration of the book from the Minda de Gunzberg Center for European Studies and the Mignone Center for Career Services at Harvard University. More recently, I've been the recipient of a wonderful fellowship at MacDowell, where I had the good luck of meeting Ken Kalfus, who graciously talked me through the reasons why I should publish this book. He was right, and I'm glad to get a score on the board.

On the topic of confidence-boosting, I must also thank Jorie Graham, whose initial response to my thesis gave me the morale to push through another few years of work, and to my agent, Katie Cacouris, who has stewarded the ship, amongst so many other things, from there.

I'm also grateful to the *Harvard Advocate*, which initially published "Master of All Subjects" under the title "Recuerdos," *Harvard Review*, which published "No Spanish," the *London Magazine*, which published "Recuerdos: Urdaibai" under the title "Urdaibai," and *Guernica*, which published "Sirens, 1985" under the title "Northern Spain, 1985." Thanks too to Laura Furman for selecting "No Spanish" for the 100th anniversary edition of *The O. Henry Prize Stories* in 2019 (Vintage Anchor).

There would be no book without my Basque family: Begoña Arrien, Arantza Arrien, Txarli Artola, Izaro Kobeaga, Aritz Arruti, Peio Kobeaga, and Sonia Gonzalez Carballo, amongst many others. Their endless generosity, patience, and warmth have made Guernica a second home, a good fortune beyond what I could have dreamed when I first visited. And, it must be said, one could have no better tour guides than Begoña and Arantza Arrien, whose knowledge of Bizkaia and its history—and whose willingness to share it—are unparalleled.

Thanks too to Aritz Branton for kindly consulting with me on the Euskera present in the book, to Mikel Garmilla for translating the Euskera in an earlier version of the story "Electrodomésticos," and to Josebe and Exkerra Latxas for sharing their home and their knowledge of shepherding with me.

I also want to acknowledge the many Basque writers whose work deals with some of the themes of this collection, and to whom I'm deeply indebted. While it would be impossible to list them all, there are some whose work is translated to English and is available in the American market, among them the wonderful Bernardo Atxaga, Kirmen Uribe, Harkaitz Cano, and Katixa Agirre.

Finally, I'm grateful to my perennial readers, Chris Alessandrini and Emma Adler, and the many other friends who offered feedback on these stories. And to my parents and brother too, who, long before they were proofreading my work, were putting up with the disappearance of all their legal pads each time a new story idea occurred to me. At last, my grandmother Madeline Marina initially sparked my interest in writing these stories with her anecdote about the peanut shells in Bilbao. I'm so thankful to her for having shared her stories with me, and I'm honored to be able to keep some of them alive in this book.

photo by Flora Hibberd

Originally from Massachusetts, Moira McCavana has spent much of her writing life responding to inherited family histories from Northern Ireland and Northern Spain. Her first published short story, "No Spanish," was selected for the 2019 O. Henry Prize anthology. Her work has appeared in *Paris Review*, *The Drift*, and *Guernica* among other places, and has been adapted to audio as an Audible Original story. In August 2022, she was the recipient of a MacDowell Fellowship.

Sarabande Books is a nonprofit independent literary press headquartered in Louisville, Kentucky. Established in 1994 to champion poetry, fiction, and essay, we are committed to creating lasting editions that honor exceptional writing. With over two hundred titles in print, we have earned a dedicated readership and a national reputation as a publisher of diverse forms and innovative voices.